Saving Grace

by Katherine Spencer

Harcourt, Inc.

Orlando Austin New York San Diego Toronto London

www.HarcourtBooks.com

Library of Congress Cataloging-in-Publication Data
Spencer, Katherine.
Saving Grace/by Katherine Spencer.
p. cm.
Summary: After her brother's death, Grace has difficulty finding meaning in her life and begins to get into various kinds of trouble, until a mysterious new girl at school helps her find her way back to family, old friends, and even God.
[1. Emotional problems—Fiction. 2. Death—Fiction. 3. Spiritual life—Fiction.]
I. Title.
PZ7.S74813Sav 2006
[Fic]—dc22 2006003639
ISBN-13: 978-0-15-205740-4 ISBN-10: 0-15-205740-4

Text set in Perpetua
Designed by Lauren Rille

First edition

H G F E D C B A

Printed in the United States of America

Saving Grace

prologue

ONE SUMMER MY BROTHER, Matt, decided he wanted to be a magician. Harry Houdini had put the idea into his head.

Actually, it was a biography of Houdini that Matt had found in the library one sticky summer afternoon. He was nine years old and I was eight. The library was the one place we were allowed to ride to on our bikes by ourselves. No matter how hot it was outside, the children's section, down a flight of cement steps, was cool and dim. The afternoon sunlight slanted in from high windows, and the large room always smelled like the musty insides of books and air-conditioning. We would ride there after lunch and stay for hours.

While I flew through the Magic Clubhouse series, unfazed by legions of drooling werewolves and slimy swamp creatures, Matt stuck to *Houdini,* studying the pages as if he would be asked to recite them word for word the first day of school.

Single-minded. That's what my father called him,

sometimes sounding proud about the trait, other times frustrated and annoyed.

Matt was definitely single-minded about becoming the *next* world's greatest magician. He'd practice in his bedroom in front of the mirror, hiding a coin in the crease between his thumb and palm, or in the tuck of his cheek. Or timing how fast he could wriggle free from a piece of rope I had knotted around his wrists.

Houdini had taught himself how to hold his breath for unbelievably long periods, a skill that came in handy when he was handcuffed, chained, straitjacketed, and locked in a metal safe submerged in the English Channel. It sounded extreme, to say the least, but I took my brother's word for it. As I did most of the time, even when we were much older.

Houdini would practice every day in the bathtub. Matt practiced in the community pool.

I'd sit on the edge, holding my mother's waterproof watch with its dark blue face and stretchy silver band. By mid-August he could stay under for a frighteningly long period.

As the seconds ticked by, worry would distract me from my job of timing him, my free hand itching to flag down one of the bored-looking lifeguards. I was only mildly reassured to see Matt's skinny arms and legs wriggling steadily beneath the chlorine blue veil.

Just when I thought I couldn't stand it a second

longer, he'd shoot up like a rocket, breaking the surface with a splash. He'd cling to the side of the pool and hang there a moment, gasping for air. Then he'd glance at me over one bony, tanned shoulder.

"Twenty-five seconds," I'd say.

He'd nod, his dark lashes spiked with water. "Just one more," he'd say.

Down he would go again before I could answer. Sometimes all I could see was the top of his dark head, his thick hair floating up, waving in the water like a sea plant.

I would wait again, watching the second hand, holding my own breath and thinking that if I allowed myself to breathe, I would jinx things somehow and he wouldn't come up again.

I would watch the seconds tick by in slow motion. Feeling my lungs grow tight, about to burst, until he broke through the surface again.

Which, of course, he always did. Eventually.

That's more or less the way I feel right now. As if he's still there, just out of sight.

In my mind I'm watching the clock, the hours passing. The days, the weeks, the months. I'm staring at the water's blue surface, rippling with sunlight, unable to breathe so I won't jinx things. Until I see him shoot up like a rocket. Smiling and victorious.

While I know it's impossible, some secret part of me

still believes that eventually, just when I think I can't stand it a second longer, there he'll be.

He'll gasp for air and laugh at my worrywart face. As if he'd purposely stayed out of sight a few seconds longer, just to tease me. Just to prove that he could.

Chapter One

PEOPLE CAN BE SO WEIRD. You think you really know somebody—your best friend or even your mom or dad—and then something happens. Something huge and unimaginable. Something that changes everything.

Afterward you realize you don't know anyone the way you thought you did.

You don't even know yourself.

That's what I kept thinking the first day of school. I'd hardly even left the house since the accident. And now, as I walked down the hallway and sat in my morning classes, everyone seemed like a stranger, giving me funny looks, whispering behind my back. Maybe I'd expected some of that. But I didn't expect people to stare right through me, as if I were invisible. As if I were the ghost, instead of Matt.

By the time lunch rolled around, I just wanted to see my friends. My mom had dropped me off late, and I'd missed meeting up with them before the first bell. The cafeteria was a complete and utter zoo, but it wasn't hard to pick my gang out of the crowd. They were sitting in the usual spot, third table down on the left, next to the courtyard windows.

"Grace! Over here!" Rebecca saw me first. She smiled and waved. When I walked over, she jumped up and slung her arms around me in a quick, tight hug. For a second I felt like my normal old self again, instead of Harding High's new sideshow, the girl whose brother had died that summer.

I dropped into a seat at the end of the table and took out my lunch. Sara Kramer was in the middle of a story, as usual, making everyone laugh.

". . . so then this *really* hot guy walks up and says, 'I can get it open. Let me try.' He yanks on the door and practically tears the locker right off the wall. I swear, he was like a superhero or something. And he was totally hot . . . Did I mention that part?" She sighed and rolled her eyes. "So I get my books out. Finally. But then I can't close the door because the Mighty Hunk has bent it totally out of shape. Now I have to go down to the office and tell somebody, and they're probably going to charge me to fix it. But the worst part is, I didn't even find out his name . . ."

She took a sip of her soda and sighed heavily. Sara is our drama queen. She can't help herself. She can leave a room for two minutes to get a drink of water and relate an entire adventure when she gets back.

"I know who you mean." Andy Chin nodded.

"Shaggy brown hair? He has on an orange T-shirt with a surf logo?"

Sara leaned across the table. "You know him?"

"He's in my chem lab. I don't think he's that hot."

"In matters of taste there can be no argument," Sara declared in an elegant tone. "And that boy is *totally* tasty."

Andy laughed and took another bite of salad. Quiet and incredibly smart, Andy never loses her cool. She always eats healthy stuff she brings from home in a plastic container and has a pin on her knapsack that says, MEAT IS MURDER.

"So, what's his name already?" Rebecca prodded.

"Rob Schneider, I think." Andy shrugged. "Something like that."

"He's not new." I shoved my half-eaten sandwich back into the plastic bag. "He transferred last spring from Ridgefield. He used to hang out with Matt sometimes."

Suddenly quiet, they all turned to look at me.

Sara looked embarrassed. "That's right. I guess I did see him around last year. Maybe he's been lifting weights over the summer . . . Grace . . . ?" Sara's blue eyes widened. She'd been so absorbed talking about her mystery man, this was the first time she'd taken a good look at me. "Whoa . . . you *totally* cut your hair. When did *that* happen?"

Andy and Rebecca exchanged swift glances. I could tell they'd noticed my hair but didn't want to make a big deal over it. I'd basically been hiding out in my room for a month and a half, ever since Matt's funeral. But the haircut was a recent development. As recent as last night, in fact. In sort of a fit, I'd just chopped it all off. I felt so different inside, I wanted it to show.

I'd done it in the bathroom with a pair of sewing scissors. My mom was in her bedroom watching TV. I could hear the sound of a home-decorating show through the half-closed door.

With Matt gone, our house felt empty and strange and lonely. Some nights I would go to my parents' room and stretch out beside my mom on the bed. We didn't really talk. We didn't have to. We each knew what the other was feeling. Other nights I'd sit on the floor in the dark hallway outside their door, wanting to be near my mother but not wanting to actually face her. Our dog, Wiley, would drop down next to me. Wiley missed Matt, too. He just couldn't say so.

Wiley and I would sit there, side by side, listening to the TV babbling away and my mom crying quietly, pulling tissues from a box on the bed, thinking no one could hear her.

Meanwhile my dad would disappear into his home office in the basement right after dinner and stay at his computer until everyone else went to bed. Sometimes I'd hear the keyboard tapping away. And other times nothing at all. He never used to work at home, but since the accident, he did it a lot.

It had been easy last night to sneak some beers out of the fridge and up to my room. I'd never had much interest in alcohol. None of my friends drank. But now I felt like, *why not?* A nice buzz sure softened the edges and helped numb the pain. I'd felt scared about coming back to school and the beers helped that, too. That's when the makeover impulse had struck, I guess.

I cried when I finally realized what I'd done. Another beer helped that, too.

After the initial shock I decided I liked the choppy look of it. It was out there. Edgy. The new Grace. So of course I had to find an outfit this morning that matched the hair, something radically different from my usual look, which was a semigrunge, no-slave-to-fashion-but-no-nerd-either style.

I'd tossed aside a T-shirt and cargo pants for a short denim skirt, then made it even skimpier using those handy scissors again. I layered a few tank tops and found a pair of awesome Indian earrings that dangled practically to my shoulders. Not quite my usual style.

This morning guys who had never given me a second look were drooling all over my history text. I didn't mind. What was the point of being so good all the time and dressing like such a nice girl, anyway? Life is short. I wanted dessert first.

Sara still stared at me.

I shrugged. "I cut it last night. I just felt like it. Guess I needed a change."

She nodded quickly. "It looks great. Honest. It's just really . . . different."

I knew she didn't like it. That's what people mean when they say "really different," right?

My poor mom had actually gagged on her coffee when I showed up in the kitchen. My father had left very early for a business conference in Baltimore, sparing me his reaction. At least until tomorrow night.

"I think it looks cool. I'd love to cut my hair. Long hair is such a pain." I could tell Andy was trying hard to be positive, because she never talked that way.

Hey, it's okay. You don't have to act all perky for me, I wanted to say.

I caught myself. It just reminded me again that I was in a bad place and my friends felt sorry for me. Maybe that was why it had been so hard to see them this last month and a half. After the funeral it was hard to see anybody.

Rebecca glanced across the table, her brown eyes soft and sympathetic. "What's your schedule like? Who did you get for trig?"

"Nurdleman. Just my luck."

Sara made a face.

"Bad break. I heard he's tough."

"The worst . . . Ma—" I tried to say more, but I couldn't get past my brother's name.

Matt, who'd been an honest-to-goodness math whiz, had promised to get me through trig, no matter what. I was certain now I'd never pass on my own.

"Did you say something, Grace?" Rebecca looked confused.

"Never mind." I shook my head. I suddenly missed the rest of my hair. The way I could conveniently hide under it. And as much as I'd wanted to see my friends, I didn't feel like sitting with them anymore. I wasn't even sure why.

"Listen, I need to take care of some stuff . . . with my guidance counselor."

"Okay, but wait a sec." Rebecca looked at Andy and Sara, and these slow, mysterious smiles appeared on all their faces.

"We have something for you. It's a surprise." Sara looked excited. She loves surprises.

I *used* to love surprises. But I didn't anymore. Surprises made me feel nervous now.

"It's a present." Andy reached under the table and pulled out a box covered with yellow gift wrap and tied with a matching satin ribbon in a professional-looking bow. You could tell it had come from some expensive shop.

She set it down in front of me. I just stared at it.

"Wow . . . why did you guys get me a present?"

They didn't say anything. We all knew why.

They were trying to cheer me up, which was really

sweet. But somehow the gesture was making me feel even worse. "You didn't have to do that."

"We know we didn't have to. We just wanted to." I could hear Rebecca struggle to keep an even, upbeat tone. "It's sort of a 'back to school' present. Didn't your mom ever get those for you?"

"Yeah, in elementary school," I said.

"My mom still gets me a cupcake from the bakery," Sara confided.

"Figures." Andy laughed.

"Don't you want to see what's inside?" Rebecca prodded me.

After a deep breath I took the gift in both hands, then slowly tore off the wrapping. Finally there was a bare white box sitting before me on the lunch table. I slowly lifted the top, my friends watching my every move.

I pulled back a few sheets of tissue paper and found a leather-bound sketchbook inside. Not the cheap kind you can buy in a stationery or art supply store. This one was a beauty, with buttery soft leather the color of rich, dark coffee and a long suede lace that wrapped around the middle of the book, secured to a silver buckle. It was just the right size, too: small enough to fit in my purse but large enough for good sketches.

"Wow, this is beautiful. I always wanted a book like this . . . You guys . . ." I shook my head, feeling like I was going to cry. Ever since I was little, I'd loved to draw and doodle. Sketching and painting is just what I like to do. Sometimes, more than anything. At times it seems the drawings just flow out of my fingers. I'd been taking art classes at the local college during the summer and sketching and painting for hours every day, but when we lost Matt, I just stopped. I still doodled a little when I was nervous or bored, but I couldn't get back to real drawing again. I wasn't sure why. I ran my hands over the smooth leather cover, wondering if the sketchbook might jump-start my battery.

"Look inside the box. There's more," Andy said.

I pushed the tissue paper back and found two slim boxes. Drawing pens imported from Sweden. My mom had bought me one last Christmas, but I'd lost it and whined about it for months.

I slipped one of the pens out of its box and saw it had been engraved: FOR FAMOUS ARTWORK. I laughed, despite feeling so choked up. I quickly opened the other box. FOR AUTOGRAPHS, read the engraving.

I struggled to swallow back the tears, not knowing what to say. I looked around at each of them. "You didn't have to do this . . . It's too much."

Sara slung an arm around my shoulders. "It was a pricey gesture, but you're worth it."

"Absolutely," Andy agreed.

Rebecca met my glance and smiled. "We want you to draw a cartoon of us for the yearbook. Remember the one you did last year?"

I smiled, remembering. "I nailed you guys perfectly."

That made them laugh. I laughed, too, and for a moment I forgot the real reason they had given me this amazing gift. For a moment it felt the way it always had. Familiar and fun. As if nothing had changed.

But everything had changed for me. My entire world had shattered. I felt close to my friends and at the same time outside the circle, watching. Connected . . . but somehow detached. Suddenly their love and sympathy, even their laughter, reminded me too much of Matt, of the way things had been before he died. I had to go.

"Hey, guys, thank you. I really love it." I stuck the box under my books and settled the pile in one arm. "I'll catch you later, right?"

Sara and Andy nodded. "See you, Grace."

"Want to get together after school? Andy and Sara are coming over to my house," Rebecca said.

"Sounds good."

I wasn't sure if I wanted to, but it seemed easier to agree and worry about it later.

We said good-bye again, and I headed off toward the vending machines for a bottle of water. I was a few steps away, digging into my pocket for some change, when I noticed Jackson Turner banging on the machine, waiting for his drink to come down.

My stomach twisted into a big knot. Jackson was the last person I wanted to see.

I did a quick 180 and headed in the opposite direction before he noticed me. Then I ducked my head and headed for the EXIT sign on the far side of the room.

I would have made it, too, if someone—and her fully loaded lunch tray—hadn't gotten in my way. It was the new girl, Philomena Cantos. As her food flipped into the air, all I saw was her shocked face, her mouth forming a perfect O of surprise.

A container of chocolate milk and the weekly special—the ingredients of Make Your Own Taco—were suddenly airborne. I jumped back in the nick of time, and most of it landed on her T-shirt and cargo pants, an outfit that looked eerily like the one I had planned to wear before my last-minute makeover.

The entire cafeteria burst out laughing. Now everyone *really* was staring at and talking about me.

I expected Philomena to start yelling or at least say something rude. But she just looked down at her splattered first-day-of-school clothes and shook her head.

"*Gross* . . . what a mess."

She dabbed at her pants with a wad of napkins, which made it even worse. I felt bad for her. The accident had definitely been my fault. Normally I would have apologized about a million times and helped her clean up.

But everyone was still laughing, and I couldn't bear to be gawked at a second longer.

"Hey, I'm sorry. But try to look where you're going next time. It might help."

She might have answered me. I'm not sure. I stepped over the mess and kept walking.

The exit was steps away. All I had to do was pass the last table, where Dana Sloan, Lindsay Wexler, and Morgan Fanning sat.

Maybe they weren't the hottest girls in the school, but they thought they were. Which was almost the same thing. They had the best hair, the best clothes, the best shoes, and the whitest teeth. They were always going skiing in Utah, shopping in New York, or spending Christmas in Antigua. Their tans knew no season.

Did I mention the jewelry? The Trinket Shack at the mall didn't cut it for these girls. They only allowed eighteen-karat gold and genuine gems to touch their skin—their idea of organic living.

I braced myself, waiting for their snide play-by-play.

Dana smiled as I walked past. "Nasty hit and run, Grace. We nearly called nine-one-one." Her friends giggled on cue.

I could have wimped out and ignored her. But I kept my cool. "Did you ever taste one of those tacos? I saved that girl's life. She should be thanking me."

Dana looked surprised. Then she laughed. "She's such a geek. Who is she?"

"I think her name's Philomena. Or something like that. She's new. She's in my gym class."

"Really."

Dana had rarely said more than two words in a row

to me during my entire life. I figured my five seconds of glory were up and I started to go.

"Hey, Grace . . . wait a sec. What's the story with that history project?" Dana rolled her eyes. "I do not get it at all."

Alphabetical order will match the most unlikely partners. Like the way Dana Sloan and I had been paired to do a term project. All Mrs. Thurber was thinking about were *S*s. It never occurred to her that Dana and I were from opposite ends of the food chain.

"It's no big deal. I'll fill you in tomorrow," I promised.

"My dad said he'll buy me a car for my birthday. But only if I keep my grades up." She sighed and smiled again.

Morgan glanced up at me. "Are you in a class together?"

"American History. Thurber," I answered.

"She's so-o-o boring, it's criminal," Dana added. "Grace made this drawing of her. It totally cracked me up."

Lindsay Wexler sat next to Dana, watching me. Her smooth dark hair and pale eyes always made me picture a cat, the kind that bites when you try to pet it. Normally Lindsay acted as if I wasn't worth talking to, but now she seemed curious. "What kind of a drawing?"

"A little doodle. Nothing special."

"Are you kidding? It's perfect. The school paper should print it, except they wouldn't dare. Let Morgan and Lindsay see it," Dana urged me. "It's really good," she promised them.

As I said before, when I get nervous or bored, I tend to doodle. Sometimes my fingers have a mind of their own and I don't even know what I'm drawing. That morning as I sat in class and Mrs. Thurber droned on about document-based questions and primary sources, my pen was scratching away.

The three of them stared at me expectantly. I pulled out my history notebook and opened it to the second page. There it was: *Portrait of Thurber. As a Cow.* With her hair in a curly perm and small, square glasses balanced on a bovine muzzle.

Dana and her friends laughed out loud. Morgan looked up at me. "I can't believe it. It looks just like her."

"I told you," Dana said.

Lindsay seemed to smile despite herself. "Pretty good."

"Really good," Dana said.

She was acting so nice, it was weird. I wondered if she felt sorry for me. Or maybe she was nicer than I thought once you got to know her a little?

"Listen, Grace, my mom's away, and a bunch of us are going to party at my house after school today," Dana said. "Want to come?"

I'd heard about hanging out at Dana's. Her parents were divorced, and her mother traveled a lot on business. Dana and her older brother, Dylan, were famous for their wild parties.

I couldn't believe I'd actually been invited to one.

She's only being nice to you because she wants you to do the history project so she can get a new car. Get it, Grace?

Yeah, I know, I answered the annoying little voice in my head. *So?*

A few months ago I would have run the other way. But that was then and this was now. Matt was gone and I was a different person.

The whole world was different.

Somehow I made it to the end of the day, dragging my tail into English Lit.

Ms. Kaplanski is a cool teacher, and English is one of my favorite subjects. We were starting the semester with *Hamlet,* she announced, and as she gave out the books, she talked about the Prince of Denmark's "major conflict": deciding things. I totally identified. Party with the cool kids for once in my life, or hang out with my comfortable, predictable best friends? That was my question.

Rebecca was in the class. She'd come in late, so we didn't get to sit together the way we usually did. When the bell rang, she waited for me up front, and we walked out into the hallway. It was so loud there, I could hardly hear myself think.

"So you're coming over today, right?" Rebecca practically had to shout. "You can take the bus with me if you want."

Part of me wanted to sink into that warm, cozy zone. Like a soak in a bubble bath. The other part felt smothered by all those sympathetic bubbles and couldn't believe I'd pass up a once-in-a-lifetime invitation to Dana Sloan's.

"I think I'll stop home first. I need to walk the dog."

"Okay, see you later." Rebecca smiled and headed for her locker.

I'd never intentionally lied to her before or purposely avoided my friends. But here I was, doing both of those things within five minutes.

I didn't understand myself lately. If I didn't want to do something, I just couldn't make myself do it. I couldn't explain it, and I didn't really give a damn if other people didn't understand. Even my best friends.

I pulled open the door to my locker and started tossing books inside.

My parents had always been on the strict side when it came to rules and curfews. But they'd gotten even worse since Matt died. They didn't know Dana and would have had strokes if they ever found out I was going to an unsupervised party.

And I didn't have Matt to cover for me now, the way we used to do for each other. Somehow that made me even more determined.

I'd be breaking the rules if I went. But part of me—a big part—didn't care. All those rules I'd tried so hard to keep. All that "should do this" and "shouldn't do that." Where had they gotten me? They hadn't kept me safe from losing Matt.

Why did something so awful happen to our family? We were all nice people who went to church and did everything we were supposed to do.

Doesn't that prove there's no God? And no point at all in trying to be so good? I do know one thing: If there is some Great Creator, CEO of the Universe up there, He or She must be pretty heartless.

I heard my cell phone and answered without checking the number.

"Hi, honey. I'm glad you picked up. Are you done with school?" My mom must have been calling from work. She sold real estate and worked at an office in town.

"I just finished."

"Great. How did it go?"

"Okay, I guess." *I'm pissed off and totally depressed and feel like the poster girl for grief. I can barely stand to be in school* would have been a more accurate report.

But my parents had it tough enough without worrying about me, too. I knew they couldn't handle my real feelings.

My real feelings would totally freak them out.

"I'm leaving work in a few minutes. Did you want to

come to the meeting at church about the homeless project? I can swing by and pick you up."

Great. I knew I should have ducked this call.

"Uh . . . I need to stay at school awhile. I'm going to join the yearbook staff. Today's the first meeting."

Lying was easier than I'd ever realized. Which was almost scary.

"Oh, okay." She sounded disappointed but didn't say anything more. I knew she thought joining the yearbook was important.

I'd been on the staff last year, and Ms. Kaplanski, our adviser, had been talking it up in class that day. I also usually went out for lacrosse with Rebecca and Sara, but I was opting out of that, too. All the extracurricular stuff that colleges love to see on your transcript seemed so boring and childish to me now.

"I'll call if I'm running late," she said. "Maybe you can start dinner. There's some chili in the fridge. You just need to warm it in the microwave."

My mother went on for a few minutes with cooking instructions. Finally we said good-bye. I dumped the phone into my backpack and realized I hadn't packed my trig text. "Nerd Man," as Matt used to call him, was already piling it on, and I couldn't afford to fall behind. I started searching through my locker again, slamming everything around.

Why did my mother have to spend so much time at church? If she wasn't out selling real estate or zoning out in front of the TV, then she was over there praying or talking to Pastor James about who-knows-what.

I tried to talk to her about it once. She said being busy helped keep her mind off Matt. Doing something worthwhile made her feel she was dedicating good work to his memory.

That all sounded very *nice*. But I just didn't get it. Why should we do any grunt work for God? God hadn't done us any favors lately.

Ever since Matt died, it felt as if my family were in a rickety boat rocking in a storm. We held on tight, fighting to keep our balance, struggling to get back to our day-to-day routines so that we wouldn't go under entirely. I forced myself to go through the motions every day and could see my parents doing the same.

I knew I shouldn't resent it if my mother had found something that helped. But anything to do with church made my stomach hurt. I felt cruelly tricked. Totally betrayed. Church seemed like one big, empty lie.

And what about me? I was still here. Didn't I need some attention? Did I have to go home to an empty house and microwave my own chili?

I finally found my trig book. It was tucked under the sweatshirt I'd worn that morning so my mom wouldn't see my outfit.

I stood up—and came face to face with Philomena Cantos.

Great. The perfect end to a perfect day.

Still, the sight of her was sort of pathetic. Her T-shirt looked tie-dyed in salsa, and the smell of tacos clung to her like a toxic cloud. I figured she'd finally worked up enough nerve to confront me, and I braced myself for what was coming.

"I think you dropped this." She held out a flyer. It was an announcement about the yearbook meeting.

I practically laughed at her. "There must be a zillion of those around school. What makes you think that's mine?"

She turned it over. There was a note written on the back. "That's your name, isn't it? Grace Stanley?"

I took the flyer from her and gave it a closer look. Ms. Kaplanski had written a note on the bottom:

Grace—
Hope to see you there. We need your wonderful drawings and special talents. If you can't make it, please drop by my office, and we'll talk.
—L. K.

"Where did you find this?"

Philomena shrugged. "I don't know. On a bench in the common, I think."

I swallowed hard. I had walked about ten miles out of my way today so that I wouldn't have to pass the common. That was where my brother had always hung out with his friends. If I walked by and didn't see Matt there, I knew I would totally lose it.

So how did this note to me from Ms. Kaplanski wind up on the common?

"Are you on the yearbook staff?" Philomena asked. "I was thinking of joining."

I sighed and stuck the flyer into my locker. "It's totally dumb and pointless. But you might like it."

"Maybe I'll try it. It sounds like fun."

This girl was weird. My sarcasm had blown right by her.

She started to go, then turned around again.

"Listen, I know I don't know you. But I just wanted to say . . . I'm sorry about your brother. I heard he was a really cool guy."

I needed a deep breath before I could speak. "Yeah. He was," I said slowly. "He was the best."

I felt my throat tighten up all of a sudden and quickly turned away from her.

She nodded and walked away. "See you, Grace."

Of all the kids who had stared at me today and whispered behind my back, she was the only one who'd had the guts to actually say something about Matt.

I finally closed my locker and spotted Dana coming out of the girls' room.

She waved and rushed toward me. "Ready? Everyone's waiting."

I slung my backpack over one shoulder while Dana tugged me toward the front entrance.

"My brother, Dylan, is parked in the traffic circle. Come on!"

I had expected to go to Dana's house on the bus, not in a car. Driven by her brother. That was another rule I'd be breaking. After Matt's accident I wasn't allowed to ride around with kids in cars much. Especially boys my parents didn't know.

The whole idea made me nervous, but I was too chicken to say so. Maybe they'd just tell me not to come.

Some kids were hanging out in front of the school, perched on the stone wall near the traffic circle. Jackson nodded at me. I ignored him and turned my back.

"Does that kid have a crush on you or something?" Dana asked.

I almost laughed at her. "No, it's nothing like that."

Dylan sat behind the wheel of a red Jeep Wrangler. The roof was off, but hey, at least there were roll bars.

Lindsay Wexler sat in front, most of her face covered by big sunglasses. But I could tell she was annoyed that she'd been kept waiting. Morgan was in the back. She turned and glanced at me. Maybe she tried to smile, but it came out more like a sneer. I scooted in next to her.

Dana hopped into the back, practically sitting in my lap, and Dylan quickly pulled out of the lot.

The backseat wasn't really big enough for three.

Luckily the car was so open, we sort of spilled out the sides. I was suddenly self-conscious about my thighs, which looked elephant-sized on the car seat next to Morgan's stick-thin legs.

I tried yanking down my skirt, but there wasn't much there to yank.

Shouting at each other above the blasting music, Dana and her friends immediately began tearing kids to shreds, mocking outfits and hair, fake tans, and cosmetic surgery.

"Did you see Brianna Whittaker's nose?" Dana laughed, hardly able to get the words out. "She ought to sue for malpractice. She looks like a troll."

Lindsay glanced at us over the top of her glasses. "It's still a big improvement, though, wouldn't you say? Considering what she used to look like."

Morgan giggled, covering her mouth with one hand. I found myself laughing, too.

Dana suddenly remembered me. She nudged my arm. "We're just having some fun. Right, guys?"

"Absolutely," Morgan shouted. "We always have fun."

I smiled back at both of them. Dylan took a sharp turn, and we suddenly shifted to one side, piling into each other as if we were on a roller coaster.

I knew I should have been nervous—worried about Dylan's driving, about my parents finding out—but I was laughing and feeling giddy from the speed and the wind rushing all around us.

Nobody knew where I was or what I was doing. I felt so free. I thought of my own friends, waiting for me, wondering what had happened. But I'd made the right choice. The one that was right for me, right now.

Chapter Two

"WHO'S READY FOR ONE of my *maravilloso* frozen margaritas?"

Dana dropped a handful of ice cubes into the blender, then hit the ON button. A furious chopping sound mixed with the music that blasted through megawatt speakers.

The Sloans' media room was unbelievable. The whole house was jaw-droppingly amazing. A three-story minimansion built of pale brick with long white columns in front, it stood on a long, sloping green lawn in the middle of one of Greenwood's best neighborhoods.

The ceilings soared, and the rooms were huge and filled with state-of-the-art . . . everything. I tried hard to act cool and not stare as Dana led us to the "family room."

Not exactly the cozy, enclosed porch we call a family room at Casa Stanley. More like a home theater and a private nightclub rolled into one.

One long wall was covered by a movie-theater-sized

projection system, another lined with several full-sized video arcade machines. The room also boasted a regulation-sized pool table. There were leather couches and chairs arranged opposite the huge TV screen, and behind the seating area was a long, shiny bar.

A genuine, bona fide bar. The kind you see in restaurants, complete with blenders, ice machines, sparkling glasses hanging from racks, and a library of liquor bottles in back. It was almost as if Dana's parents were begging us to drink.

Morgan and Lindsay had strolled in and immediately flopped onto the leather couches, kicking off their shoes.

Dylan had gone straight to the remote, finally settling on a music video channel. He turned the volume so high, I felt the floor vibrate.

Dana poured the drinks into cocktail glasses with long stems, a crust of salt clinging to the rims. "To surviving the first day of school. Who wouldn't need a drink after that?"

She raised her glass, and when we all clinked together, I felt I was really part of things. Like I might actually become part of their group.

Morgan and Lindsay watched as I took my first sip. I'd never had a frozen margarita before, but I was determined not to let it show.

Not a problem, I decided. It tasted sweet and salty at the same time, a little tart.

"This is just what I needed." I took another enthusiastic swallow.

"Don't chug that down too fast, sweetie. It's not Gatorade." Lindsay laughed at me, but I just ignored her. I saw her look at Morgan again to share another sneer, but Morgan was carefully studying the nutritional information on the back of the bottle of cocktail mix.

"Oh, my god. This stuff is *loaded* with carbs. All that sugar . . . ugh!"

She stared at her drink as if it had been poisoned. I wondered if she was going to run into the bathroom to throw up.

Dylan had disappeared for a few minutes but now returned with a guy I vaguely recognized from school, Ben Kruger. Ben and Dylan both played varsity basketball.

Lindsay got up to dance, swinging her hips and swishing her long dark hair around as if she were in a shampoo commercial. She pulled Morgan up, and they danced together, backlit by the giant TV.

The guys stood by the bar watching, tipping their heads back to slug their beers out of the bottle. Ben leaned over and whispered something to Dylan, and they both cracked up.

Despite Lindsay's warning, or maybe because of it, I took a few more gulps of my drink, draining it to the bottom. Dana filled my glass again. "Come on, Grace.

Time to dance." I didn't really want to, but she wouldn't give up.

I got up, feeling my head spin. The music was deafening, the only light in the room coming from the flashing images on the giant TV.

I danced around, feeling self-conscious. I sipped my drink, some of it sloshing onto my clothes. I just hoped it didn't stain or leave me smelling like a margarita when I got home.

How was I going to get home, anyway? Was Dylan going to drive me, after he'd been drinking beer all afternoon?

Having fun yet? a little voice inquired.

Loads of it. Shut up and go away.

Someone took me by the hand and spun me around. It was Dylan. I put my drink down and followed his moves. He wasn't a bad dancer.

He leaned over and spoke into my ear. "This is a really good song."

I nodded. He was so close, I felt his breath on my ear.

I'd only heard the tune a few times before. It was some new indie band. Matt would have known. He knew more about music than anybody. I'd depended on him to keep me up on the hot bands and new songs; lately I didn't have a clue.

I took another look at Dylan. He was flat-out gorgeous. And he knew it. He had a great face and thick brownish blond hair he wore long in front, flopping across his eyes. Of course I'd noticed him around school before. You'd have to be dead not to.

It was fun to have him notice me. A lot of girls in school would have traded in their iPods just to dance with him.

Like Lindsay, for instance.

She wriggled over to us, edging me aside. Her faded, artfully shredded jeans sat impossibly low on her hips, a tooled leather belt barely holding them in place. She danced with her arms waving in the air above her head, bracelets jangling, and the hem of her tunic top climbing up over her ribs.

She tossed her hair around, really into the music. Or acting as if she was. I ducked to avoid getting smacked in the face. Dylan laughed and finally started dancing with her, too.

Where had I seen this type of dancing before? Maybe on Animal Planet? She was definitely "defending her territory." Mostly, I thought her play for Dylan was so obvious, it was pathetic.

I danced around some more, surveying the scene as one video merged with the next. Dana danced with Ben off in a corner, his hands sliding up and down her body. Morgan had settled cross-legged on the floor, talking on her cell phone, her bony legs jutting up at odd angles.

My margarita sat in a puddle on the slate coffee

table. I took a few sips, then suddenly craved a plain old drink of water.

It seemed too embarrassing to get some from the bar, even though I'd seen water bottles in the fridge below the counter. Besides, if Lindsay caught me drinking anything but liquor, I'd probably never hear the end of it.

I slipped upstairs and went in search of the kitchen. It wasn't hard to find. It was also stadium-sized, the cabinets made of glossy wood; the countertops, black granite. Huge, stainless-steel appliances lined the walls, including a long, industrial-sized fridge with glass sliding doors—the fridge looked big enough to double as a guest room.

I opened one side of it and found a bottle of spring water, then drank it down without stopping.

"It's the salt. And the sugar, too. Makes you too thirsty. That's why I stick with the hops."

Dylan stood in the doorway and held up his beer bottle.

I wasn't sure if he'd followed me or had just gotten bored with Lindsay. I put the empty water bottle on the countertop. He was holding an extra beer in his other hand and tossed it to me.

"Think fast."

I grabbed for the bottle, catching hold of it just before it slipped to the floor.

He laughed. "Good reflexes."

"Thanks."

I didn't really want the beer, but I thought, *why not?* One couldn't hurt me. I liked the beer better than the sweet blender drinks, anyway.

I twisted off the top and sipped the quickly rising foam. It was not smart to toss around a bottle of beer before you drank it. Even I knew that.

Dylan watched me, looking pleased. "That's more like it, right?"

"Absolutely."

He stepped over and leaned against the counter next to me. "At least you didn't ask if it was a lite."

"I don't really like lite beer. I like . . . heavy beer."

Dylan laughed, though he didn't understand the real joke. It was this dumb fake commercial Matt had made up while watching all the lite beer ads during a baseball game.

"Heavy beer!" Matt would shout, slipping into a super twangy, down-home, western accent. "That's what *real* men drink, fella. Not that sissy stuff. Heavy beer fills you up! *And* out! Three times more carbs and a barnful of calories! Brewed in the wi-i-i-de open spaces . . . where we don't give a dang how big we get!"

Matt would stuff a couch pillow under his T-shirt, making a big beer belly, then run around the room, punctuating his act with fake belches.

When he got too crazy, my mother would come in and tell him to stop. But he'd just get worse, and she'd start laughing, too.

I guess you had to be there.

I must have looked a little distracted while this old home movie flashed through my mind.

Dylan stared down at me. "You don't feel sick or anything, do you?"

I shook my head. "I'm okay . . . I was just thinking about something."

He nodded and took another swig of his beer. Then he looked at me and flipped his hair out of his eyes. "Want to come up to my room?"

I took a breath. "Okay."

He grabbed my hand and led me through the house, out to the huge foyer and up a staircase that curved around the way the stairs in the movies always do.

We walked down a long hallway. All the doors were closed, painted glossy white with big brass doorknobs. The walls were the color of coffee ice cream, the floors slick, polished wood. Black-and-white photos in thick black frames hung on the walls.

I stopped to look at one, a grainy, abstract landscape that could have been taken on the moon. Except that Dylan and Dana were standing in the far distance, wearing shorts and T-shirts and carrying packs.

"My mom took those on vacation last year. We were hiking in Hawaii, on the lava fields."

"Is your mother a photographer?"

He laughed. "Hell, no. She's a lawyer. She works for an investment firm."

He said it in a way that made me feel dumb for asking. Then he opened a door and cocked his head at me. "Come on in. Sorry it's trashed. Our housekeeper took the day off."

He followed me inside and shut the door behind us.

Late-afternoon sunlight filtered through wooden slat shades that covered the long windows. I saw a large aquarium where brightly colored fish darted from side to side. There was a hutch with a corner desk, where a notebook computer sat. And a big bed with a dark, gray-blue quilt half hanging onto the floor.

The wall opposite the bed was covered by rows of shelves. There were some books but mostly sports trophies and plaques. I walked closer and took a better look. It seemed as if Dylan had saved every acknowledgment of his athletic talents since kindergarten, starting with peewee soccer.

When I turned, he was watching me, his arms crossed loosely over his chest, his muscles showing through his T-shirt. I hadn't been invited into too many bedrooms by boys, but for some reason I wasn't nervous. Maybe because it was so unreal, almost like a dream, being invited to Dylan Sloan's bedroom. Maybe because I wasn't sure yet if I really liked him. Or maybe because of the margaritas.

Last year there was this guy I really liked, Zach Tobin. I'd had this ridiculous crush on him since middle school. We worked on the yearbook together, and we finally went out for a while. He was the complete opposite of Dylan—about my height, with dark hair and eyes, fast talking, and funny. It was an ego boost to have somebody you'd always had a crush on start asking you out.

But after Matt died, I didn't feel the same about Zach anymore. He tried to understand what I was going through, but I knew he never could. I felt so distant from him. He was still part of the normal world, and I was part of a new select club: people who've had someone die on them. Two and a half weeks after the funeral I told him we had to break up. I hardly even thought about him anymore.

"Those are all my trophies," Dylan said.

"You have a ton of them. Lots of dusting for your mom," I teased.

He laughed at me. "My mom never dusts. I don't think she knows how."

He stepped over to me and took down a large, shiny trophy. He held it out carefully in both hands. I sensed this collection really mattered to him. It wasn't something he joked about.

"This is from the county finals last year. I was MVP."

"Pretty good. I don't watch our school teams much. I must have missed that one."

He shrugged, still looking at the trophy. "Maybe you'll watch me play this year. We're going all the way. State champions."

"What position do you play?"

He laughed, as if everyone knew that. "Varsity power forward. Do you know what that is?" He rested his hands on my shoulders then ran them up and down my bare arms.

"Sure, I know." I didn't move any closer.

He didn't say anything, just looked down at me for a long time, stroking my arms, then massaging my shoulders. "How come I never noticed you around school before?"

Because we live on different planets?

"Maybe you don't recognize me. My hair used to be much longer." I ran my fingers through my freshly chopped hair.

I couldn't believe it. Dylan Sloan was putting the moves on me . . . in his bedroom!

"I like your hair. It's cool." He reached up and touched my short hair, fluffing it with his fingers. "So are you."

"Thanks."

He leaned over and kissed me then, just grazing my mouth. His lips were surprisingly soft, and his mouth tasted of beer. But mine did, too, I guess.

I kissed him back, feeling a little dizzy and foggy-headed.

He pulled me closer, his arms sliding around my body, his hands rubbing my back. His touch felt good, warm and strong. And he was so hot. Who could resist?

"Mmm. You taste good," he whispered before kissing me again, this time a bit harder, more insistent.

I opened my mouth and felt his tongue slide inside. This kiss went on for what seemed like a long time. Dylan slowly led us across the room toward his bed. Finally I felt the edge of the mattress bump the back of my legs, and I pulled back my head.

"Come on, just sit down with me." He had one arm around my waist and tugged me down next to him. We started kissing again, harder and faster. I fell back on the bed, and he covered me, one hand moving under the edge of my shirt on the bare skin of my stomach.

I put a hand over his, stopping him, and his eyes opened. He didn't say anything at first, just looked down at me.

"Something wrong?"

I shook my head. "No. I'm okay."

He stared at me a moment. I felt his weight pressing me into the mattress. "Hey, I really like you, you know?"

"Thanks . . . I like you, too."

"You do?"

I nodded. "Sure."

"Okay, then. Don't worry. Nothing's going to happen that you don't want."

I nodded again. "Okay."

He quickly dipped his head and started kissing me again. I thought for a moment of pushing him away and getting up. This was happening sort of fast for me.

But I liked the feeling of his kissing me, touching me. For a moment it made me forget . . . everything.

I kissed him back willingly and felt his hand wander under my shirt again. As soon as I'd put my head down, the margaritas and beer hit me, making my head spin. Everything seemed to be happening to me at a distance. Even Dylan seemed to be far away somehow.

What would Matt have thought about this scene? He would have teased me mercilessly if he'd ever known I was making out with the MVP of the basketball team.

I squeezed my eyes shut, and for a moment, for some crazy reason, I felt like crying.

Matt was gone. It didn't matter.

Nothing mattered now.

We kissed some more. It felt good. It felt real. Dylan ran his hands up and down my body, then pushed up my shirt.

Suddenly the door burst open. We both sat up, startled. It was Dana. I jumped up, not sure what she'd seen—though I was certain she grasped the basic concept.

"Quick! Gloria . . . she's coming up the driveway!"

Dana ran down the hallway again, and Dylan jumped up, too. He grabbed our empty beer bottles and tossed them under his bed.

"Come on, you go into Dana's room. Act cool, like you were already in there talking."

"Who's Gloria? Is that your housekeeper?"

"Our stepmother. She and my dad live across town. It's not even his night. I have no idea what she's doing here."

He led me down the hallway and into another bedroom. This one was decorated in periwinkle blue and white with a loft bed and built-in furniture. Morgan sat in a leather armchair, Lindsay on a bentwood rocker.

Lindsay's eyes slid over me. "So, did you enjoy the tour of Dylan's room? Did you get to see his *big* trophy?" She flashed me an acid smile. "Pretty impressive, right?"

I didn't answer. I felt my face getting hot and red.

Lindsay turned to Morgan. "I don't think he showed it to her yet."

"Maybe they didn't have time," Morgan said.

I couldn't tell if Morgan was as venomous as Lindsay or was just sort of lost. Low blood sugar and all that. Before we could get into it any further, Dana rushed in.

"Everybody, take a mint, quick!" She tossed me a tin of Breath Blasters. I popped two into my mouth and passed them along. They burned my tongue and tasted like medicine, but I chewed them up anyway.

Morgan sat reading the back of the package.

Dana yanked open her backpack and tugged out some books, then spread them around the floor. She dropped onto the carpeting and put a book in her lap. "Remember, we've just been sitting around, talking about school."

"Dana, your blouse is buttoned wrong," Morgan said quietly.

"Oh . . . damn—" She fumbled to quickly rebutton her shirt.

I heard a brisk knock on the bedroom door, and it suddenly opened.

"Dana, are you in here?" A tall, slim woman strode into the room on pencil-thin high heels. Her suit was simple and sleek, her big earrings and bracelet made of jagged chunks of gold. She frowned down at us, her smooth, reddish brown hair falling toward her chin at an angle. "Didn't you hear me calling?"

Dana shrugged. "Nope . . . Have you been here long?"

"Long enough." Gloria looked down at her stepdaughter, unsmiling.

"Why are you here? It's not Friday," Dana said.

Gloria's head tilted back. "Your father had to switch his night. He called your mother and worked it all out."

"She forgot to tell us, I guess," Dana said. "Do we have to go with you?"

"What kind of question is that?" Gloria's tone was thin and sarcastic. She quickly glanced around at the rest of us.

"Hello, Mrs. Sloan." Lindsay offered one of her fake, sugary smiles. Morgan smiled, too. Hers was probably noncaloric sweetener, though.

When Gloria's gaze finally reached me, I felt as if she could see right into my brain. My poor, abused stomach churned with margaritas and beer, and my mouth felt as dry as cotton.

"Hi, I'm Grace." My hand popped up in a nervous, puppetlike gesture.

"Grace is in my history class," Dana piped up. "We're doing a project together."

Gloria crossed her arms over her chest. She didn't seem to be buying any of this. "Where's your brother?"

Dana shrugged. "In his room, I think."

"I just looked. He's not there."

Dana feigned another innocent stare. "Maybe he's downstairs? Playing video games?"

Gloria's brown eyes narrowed. "You mean, maybe he's in the garage, hiding the empties."

Dana looked confused, then amused. "Doing *what?*"

"May I speak to you out in the hall a minute, please?"

Dana sighed and slowly rose. "Be right back, guys."

We looked at one another but didn't say anything. Even Lindsay didn't have a smart remark.

I sat closest to the door and could hear Dana and Gloria talking in the hallway. ". . . Do you think I was born yesterday? I heard the music blasting from two blocks away."

Dana started to reply, but Gloria's voice drowned her out again. "Oh, really? Well, I don't believe you. Your mother is going to hear about this. She lets the two of you get away with murder."

Dana spoke again, very softly. "We were just hanging out, talking about school—"

"Pack up. You and Dylan are coming back to spend the night."

A few moments later Dana returned, looking glum and defeated. "Sorry, guys, you have to go. Gloria's going to drop everyone home."

She pulled a duffel out of her closet and started tossing clothes inside. "I have to see my stupid father. Ugh. He's such a jerk." She made a face and mock-stuck a finger down her throat.

Lindsay and Morgan laughed. But I felt sorry for her.

Dana's mother didn't seem to be in line for any parenting awards, either. As for Gloria, she appeared to be the Wicked Witch in Pradas.

Morgan sat chewing on a strand of her hair. "Do you think she'll call our parents?"

"What would she say? She didn't really see anything," Dana whispered back. She tossed a hairbrush into her bag and zipped it up. "Gloria talks tough, but she's afraid to make me and Dylan mad at her."

"Dana? Are you ready? I'm waiting in the car," Gloria called up the stairway. "We have a six-thirty reservation at Fusion Grille."

"Big deal," Dana answered in a voice only we could hear. "I'm so sick of Pan-Asian."

Carrying our backpacks, we followed Dana into the hall and down the stairs. Gloria drove a long, black luxury SUV with three rows of plush leather seats and all the extras, including a flat-screen monitor hanging from the ceiling. The radio was set to an all-news station, and when Dana tried to change it, Gloria barked at her.

Dylan sat up front, and I found a place in back. He glanced at me a few times, but we were too far away to speak to each other.

I sat by a window and stared out at the streets flowing past. It was almost dark. I hoped my mother wasn't home yet. I smelled of beer and looked totally trashed. Even she would have guessed I hadn't stayed after school for a yearbook meeting.

What if Dana's stepmother called? My parents would flip out.

Get a grip, Grace. Gloria isn't going to call. Dana promised. Besides, even if she tries, Mom will be at church, and Dad will be hiding in the basement.

When it was my turn to be dropped off, I gave Gloria directions into my neighborhood. The windows of the houses glowed, warm yellow squares. Families were gathering for dinner, talking about their days. Parents were telling kids to finish their homework, set the table, walk the dog.

Just another weeknight, the regular routines taken for granted, as if everyone would always be together and nothing would ever change.

They didn't realize. How could they? It had to happen to you. Then you knew.

If Gloria called, well . . . it wouldn't be the end of the world.

I'd already been to the end of the world. I'd been there and back.

❦

Luckily I got home before my mother. I took Wiley out for a quick walk, then ran upstairs, pulled off my clothes, and took a shower.

The house seemed so empty and dark. I used to enjoy being alone at home. I never minded the solitude. But now the silence made me think too much, remember too much. I pulled on some sweats and a big T-shirt and slipped my feet into fluffy slippers.

I tried to ignore Matt's room as I headed downstairs, but it was impossible. My mother kept the door closed. She only went in to vacuum and dust. I opened the door a crack and peeked inside. It looked dark and shadowy. A little spooky.

I walked in and switched on a low light by his bed. Everything was perfectly tidy, way neater than the way he'd kept it.

His three guitars, two electric and one acoustic, were set up on stands near his desk. His books were lined up on the shelves, his CD collection in stacks by the far wall, next to an amp and some piles of music. A poster from some indie band hung lopsided on the wall; the tape at the corners had all but dried up.

I wondered if I should fix it or just let it fall off when it was ready. Like an autumn leaf on a tree. I squeezed my eyes shut, my fingers digging into the quilt. "Matt . . . where the hell are you? Why don't you just . . . just come home already, okay?"

I heard Wiley run into the room, and I realized I'd been talking out loud. The dog stopped in the middle of the room and stared at me. "It's okay," I said quietly. "Don't mind me."

Wiley walked over and licked my hand. I sighed and patted his head. "Yeah. You're right. Time to start dinner."

I clicked off the light and shut the door. We went downstairs, and I gave Wiley his can of dog food. A gross job, but somebody had to do it now.

I scanned the fridge and pulled out the chili. The dog food almost looked good in comparison. But I dutifully dumped the chili into a bowl and covered it up, then jabbed some buttons on the microwave, hoping I didn't incinerate it.

Or maybe hoping I did, so we could order takeout.

Then I pulled out a box of rice and studied the directions for a while. The silence in the house seemed deafening. Why did I have to get stuck doing this homemaker routine? Why wasn't my mother back yet? For all she knew, I could have been home hours ago, hanging out here all alone. What was so god-awful important at church that she couldn't even come home for her own daughter?

The only kid she had left, I might add.

I was so furious, I skipped the directions entirely. I poured some water into the pot, dumped in some rice, and turned the heat up really high. I was certain that wasn't the right way to cook the stuff, but I didn't care.

I thought about having a beer, but my head ached from the happy hour at Dana's, so I wound up taking some aspirin and drinking a glass of iced tea instead. I sifted through the mail and found a good magazine. I already had tons of homework, but I didn't want to deal with any of it.

When my mom walked in, I was deep into an article about exfoliating your skin. I had definitely fallen behind on the skin-care routine and needed some quick tips to catch up now that Dylan was in the picture.

"Been home long?"

"A little while." I watched as she dropped a bag of groceries onto the counter.

"I'm sorry I'm so late. Thanks for starting dinner." She quickly washed her hands and started setting the table. I was mad at her for staying at church so long, but I was also happy to see her. Finally.

She took out some lettuce for a salad and rinsed it in the sink.

"So, how was school? How was your first day?" Under her upbeat tone I heard her feeling anxious for me.

"It was okay."

"Do you like your teachers?"

"Yeah, I guess." I shrugged.

"Do you have Ms. Kaplanski again? She's good, right?"

"Yup. One decent class." I was about to add that I'd pulled Nurdleman for trig but caught myself. Matt had complained constantly about Nerd Man, and I didn't want to remind her. "I made some rice, but I think it burned on the bottom," I said.

She peeked under the pot cover, then turned down the burner. "It looks fine."

She chopped a tomato and dropped it into the salad, then made some dressing. "Did you get Mrs. Wolf for art this year?"

I didn't answer right away. "I'm not taking art," I said finally.

She turned to look to me, then back at the salad. "Really? I'm surprised. I thought you got into the advanced class."

"I couldn't fit it into my schedule."

That was like saying I couldn't fit breathing into my schedule. My mother knew it. I readied myself for an argument.

She shook her head. "That's too bad. Maybe next semester."

"Maybe," I replied.

She worked without saying anything but kept glancing over at me, a tactic I knew she'd heard about on a talk show: "Five Surefire Ways to Get Your Teen to Talk!"

A helpful shrink who had written a book all about it

advised parents to "create a vacuum in the dialogue," which the child is then "tempted to fill."

I wasn't falling for it.

We put the food onto the table and sat down. My mother glanced over at me. "Let's say a blessing, okay?"

She didn't wait for me to answer, just bowed her head and began. "Thank you, Lord, for all we have received this day from your bounty. We are grateful for this meal and the love around this table. Please bless everyone at this table, and everyone in our family who isn't with us tonight."

By that she meant my father, I guessed. And maybe Matt, too.

I stared at my plate until she was done but didn't fold my hands or anything prayerful like that. I'd never really minded when my parents said a blessing before a meal. I'd grown up that way, and it seemed normal to me. But now I could barely stand to hear them thanking God for anything, no matter how brief or insipid they tried to keep it.

"How did everyone like your hair?"

"Nobody said anything."

"Nobody?"

"Just Sara. Oh, and some guy said he thought it looked cool."

I was thinking of Dylan, of course.

My mom gave me a long look, then started eating again. "I think you look very nice with short hair. Not everyone can wear it, you know. It shows off your pretty face."

I rolled my eyes. "Thanks, Mom."

"The last time you had hair that short, you were about five. You got a huge wad of gum stuck right in the back, and there was nothing we could do except get it all cut off. Remember?"

Matt had stuck the gum there, but she didn't seem to remember that part—or was conveniently revising history.

I stabbed a bite of chili with my fork. "Yeah, I remember."

"I'm getting used to it."

"That makes one of you. Dad is going to have a stroke."

"He's prepared. I already told him."

Just the words, the way she said them, made me think of Matt again. About the night the state troopers knocked on our door. Two of them, a matched set. My mom was home, but my dad was still at work. Matt had gone out with the car a short time before, to get a container of milk. A dog or something had run in front of the car, and Matt had swerved off the road and driven into a tree. At least, that was the most anyone could piece together.

My mother knew she couldn't tell my father about the accident, and she'd asked the troopers to stay, to help her break the news to him.

Now she seemed nervous, restless. She took another spoonful of rice onto her plate, though it was mostly burned and tasted pretty dreadful. "How did the meeting go?" she asked quietly.

Meeting? She's the one who went to a meeting. Then I remembered my lie about the yearbook.

"Oh . . . okay. It was just sort of an information meeting. I'm not sure if I'm going to join again."

"You did some great illustrations last year. I thought you were in line to be the art editor. That would look good on your college applications," she reminded me.

I shrugged. "I don't know. I'm not sure."

Actually, I *was* sure I didn't want to do any clubs or sports this year, but I didn't feel like talking about it right now.

Then my mom gave me what Matt and I used to call one of her *significant* looks. Her head sort of tilts to the side, and her eyebrows knit together, making a little crease in her forehead.

Matt used to do a perfect imitation. I nearly glanced over at his empty chair for a "look alert" . . . then caught myself.

"Is it because of Zach?"

"Zach? What does he have to do with it?"

"Is he on the yearbook again, and you don't want to see him?"

Sometimes my mom can be *so* off base, it's scary. Who even cared if Zach Tobin lived on the planet?

Especially after the afternoon I'd had in Dylan Sloan's bedroom.

"That is so over. I can't believe I ever went out with him."

She took a long breath and sat back in her seat. "Okay. I was just wondering."

She looked at me but didn't say anything. It was because of Matt. Not Zach. She knew it, and so did I.

I looked at my plate and pushed the food around with my fork.

"The meeting at church went really well. A lot more people showed up than I expected. A lot of kids you know from the youth group came. Jackson Turner was there," she added.

Jackson. Maybe that's why he'd been chasing me around today. He was trying to sign me up for this charity project, too. He needed serious help, no doubt about it.

When I didn't say anything, she added, "They had some good ideas about how to raise money. They want to have a concert . . . with local bands."

Her voice sort of cracked on the last part. I stared at her. "Local bands? As in rock bands?"

My mother pursed her lips and nodded. "That's right."

Matt had been part of a band. It was just about all he lived for. Matt had started the group with Jackson, his best friend. Matt played bass and sang, wrote songs, and even thought up their name, The Daily Dose.

My brother was such a ham. He loved being onstage, the center of attention. Mom always said she must have eaten too much bacon when she was pregnant with him.

He would have loved playing in a big concert at our church. There wouldn't have been any living with him. But he would never make music again. He would never run around the stage and act out or bask in the roar of applause.

And if he couldn't play anymore, I couldn't stand to hear about other kids who could.

I stared at my mother. It seemed such . . . such a betrayal that she'd take part in this. Didn't she see that?

"Grace, don't be angry. Nothing's been decided. It's only a suggestion."

"But you would think that was all right, if that's what they decide to do? I mean, you'd help out and still be a volunteer and all that?"

I didn't mean to shout at her, but my voice grew louder and angrier with every word.

"Grace, please. I know what you're thinking." She reached across the table and tried to touch my arm.

I pulled away. "Sorry. *Wrong.* You don't have a *freaking* clue. If you knew one tiny bit, you'd never go anywhere near this stupid concert idea."

“But it’s not just my decision, Grace. I’m part of a committee . . .”

I jumped up from my seat. “So? Nobody’s forcing you.”

She glanced at me, then looked away. Her eyes had filled with tears.

“No, no one is forcing me. That’s true.” She took a long breath. I saw her hands pressed together in her lap. “I do have my reasons for being part of this, Grace . . . I know you don’t really understand.”

A tear slid down her cheek. She whisked it aside with her fingers then wiped her nose with a paper napkin.

I didn’t know what to say. I wanted to scream. But I couldn’t even breathe.

I stomped up to my room and slammed the door. Then I threw myself facedown onto my bed and cried.

A long time later I heard the TV in my mother’s room. I walked down the hall and nearly sat on the floor outside the doorway. Finally, I poked my head in.

My mother was watching a cooking show. A hip-looking chef was poking chicken parts in a frying pan with long silver tongs, yelling at the audience in an Australian accent.

My mother sat propped against her pillow, wearing her flowered robe. She looked tired and sad. She glanced at me and patted the space beside her. I walked over and slipped onto the bed next to her. She hugged me with one arm around my shoulders, then buried her face in my neck for a minute.

I curled up next to her, and she stroked my short hair.

My mom was crying again but didn't stop to wipe her eyes.

"I'm sorry, sweetie." Her voice was so soft, I could hardly hear it.

She might have been talking about the concert. Or maybe about Matt. I wasn't sure.

Either way, I knew what she meant.

"I know," I whispered back. "It's not your fault."

Chapter Three

WHEN I GOT TO SCHOOL the next morning, Rebecca was on the front lawn, waiting for the first bell to ring. I felt a pang of guilt about the way I'd stood up my friends. But I didn't regret going to Dana's house.

I could tell that Rebecca was annoyed. She had that pinched look she gets when her feelings are hurt. I'd seen that look since second grade, and for some reason this morning it really bugged me.

"Sorry I didn't make it over to your house yesterday," I said. "I was going to call but . . . I got into this big thing with my mother."

I *had* argued with my mother, so it wasn't entirely a lie, was it?

Rebecca shrugged. "No big deal. What happened with your mom?"

"There's this thing going on at church, and she wants me to help out . . . It's hard to explain."

"Oh, okay." Rebecca picked up her knapsack and lacrosse stick and headed for the building. I walked beside her. I hadn't been a very reliable friend lately, but

Rebecca and the others had been cutting me an unlimited amount of slack. She seemed to be sticking to that policy.

I spotted Dylan at the end of the hall, but he didn't see me. Which was fine. I wasn't ready yet to face him. I didn't know how I should act, what I should say. I'd never gotten drunk and made out with a guy the first time we'd met.

I was dying to tell Rebecca about it. I so wanted to see the look on her face. But I couldn't tell her. I didn't want her to know I'd lied about where I'd been after school the day before.

"Want to get together this afternoon?" I said. "You can come to my house."

"Can't. Lacrosse tryouts. We won't be done until late."

She hadn't even asked if I was trying out this year. I guess it was obvious. Practice had started last week, and I hadn't gone to any of the workouts.

"Too bad you're not going out for the team. We're going to be awesome." She sounded sad, and suddenly I was, too.

"I just got lazy, I guess." Or was lacrosse something else I'd outgrown while Rebecca was still into it? One afternoon at Dana's house, and I'd begun to wonder about my friendship with Rebecca. It was starting to feel like a favorite old sweater that didn't fit anymore.

"How about Friday?" Rebecca jammed her stick into her locker and slammed the door. "I'm sitting for the Delaney kids. I should be done by dinnertime. We could get together then."

"Friday should be okay." I wondered if I should commit and risk missing out on an invite from Dana. But Rebecca misread the hesitant note in my voice.

"I didn't mean to steal your job, Grace, but Mrs. Delaney said you gave her my number."

"No problem. It's cool. I told her to call you, didn't I?"

The Delaneys had moved in down the street from us about two years ago and had been my regular babysitting job ever since. They had two kids. Ruthie was five, going on thirty-five, and Sam was three. They were cute and easy to handle most of the time, and for some reason they sort of worshipped me. I did miss them. But they didn't understand what had happened to Matt and had a knack for asking me these excruciatingly honest "kid" questions that always put me back to square one. So, lately, whenever Mrs. Delaney called, I said I was busy and recommended she call Rebecca. She must have given up on me.

Rebecca pushed her hair back with one hand. Her brownish red hair was parted on the side today and curling from the humidity. I thought she had great hair, but she always wished it was stick straight, like mine.

"I'll walk down to your house when I'm done at the

Delaneys'," she offered. "We can get sushi or something. How about Andy and Sara? Maybe they'd want to come, too."

"Good idea." I nodded. "I'll ask them."

The bell rang, and we headed for first period. Rebecca looked pleased we'd made plans. But I was thinking that Friday night sushi sounded pretty dull compared to my afternoon at Dana's house.

My first class was history, and Dana was already sitting in a front row seat. "Hey, Grace," she said as I dropped into the empty seat next to hers. "How's your head feeling?"

"I'm good. How did dinner turn out? Your stepmother seemed pretty annoyed."

"She complained a lot about us to my dad. But he never does anything." She made a face. "We have to stay with them until my mother gets back from L.A., which totally sucks."

"Too bad."

This was going to put a major crimp in Dana's social life. There wouldn't be any after-school parties at Gloria's house, that was for sure. And just when I was starting to be included in the inner circle.

Then she smiled slyly. "You and Dylan seemed really into each other yesterday. Or was that just the tequila?"

More like that last beer Dylan had tossed me in the kitchen.

But I really liked him. More than I'd ever expected. I practically couldn't stop thinking about him all last night and this morning. I could hardly believe he liked me. Everyone thought Dylan Sloan was hot. Even my friends, who assumed all rich, popular superjocks were idiots.

Being around Dylan was . . . uncomplicated. There wasn't heavy history to deal with. I didn't feel as if he was looking at me and thinking of Matt all the time. Which was a relief.

Dana leaned closer. "I think he's going to ask you out," she confided.

"He is? I'd go out with him in a minute."

Nothing like playing it cool, Grace.

"Thought you'd say that." Her smile was smug, suggesting I'd have to be crazy if I didn't want to go out with her older brother. But I couldn't blame her. I'd felt the same about my older brother.

The bell rang, and Mrs. Thurber shut the door. A few stragglers scrambled for seats, like in a round of musical chairs. She ignored them and started passing out printed sheets.

"I know you'll all be thrilled to receive this morning's handout," she began. "It lists the requirements for your term project. As you can see, different stages are due on different dates. This should help you organize your time. I'm only going to warn you once: This isn't the type of project you can rush to do in one night or even over a weekend."

I glanced at the sheet. No wonder Mrs. Thurber had paired us up. It would definitely take more than one person to complete this amount of work. Groups of ten would have been ideal.

"... consider yourselves history detectives," she continued, sounding slightly less robotic. "You're going to root out those primary sources—letters, diaries, photographs, newspaper articles—and draw your own conclusions."

At least the project sounded interesting. I like reading old letters and journals and I love looking at old photographs.

I glanced at my partner. Dana was playing with her bracelet, arranging the charms in different positions on her wrist.

"Who knows? Maybe one of you will make a valuable historic discovery. I just read in the newspaper a few weeks ago that a high school student near Columbus uncovered a cache of letters written by Warren G. Harding. Can you imagine *that*?"

Dana turned to me and made a face. I rolled my eyes in answer.

Of course Mrs. Thurber picked that exact moment to look at me. "Any questions, Grace?"

I shook my head, my eyes suddenly big and innocent. "Um, no . . . not really."

"Well, when you really have one, get back to me, dear."

Mrs. Thurber rattled on about primary sources, practically quivering with excitement every time she said the words. Then she announced that the class would adjourn to the library for the rest of the period, so we could begin narrowing down our topics. A thesis statement was due next Tuesday.

Dana and I strolled toward the library as if we had all week to get there.

"Maybe we should start by checking out the Nineteenth Amendment to the Constitution," I said. "There's probably a lot of letters and journals written by the suffragettes, and it definitely fits into the time period she asked for."

Dana gave me a blank look.

"The Nineteenth Amendment gave women the right to vote?" I reminded her.

"Oh . . . right. I knew that." She shrugged and tossed her hair over her shoulders. "Hey, you pick out the topic if you really want to, Grace. I'm cool with that."

Then she gave me a big encouraging smile. Her teeth were so white, it was almost unnatural. But not in an unattractive way.

We were passing the common. A guy waved and smiled at Dana. I didn't know his name, but I was pretty sure he hung out with Dylan and played on the basketball team. He was seriously cute.

Dana fluffed up her hair with her fingertips and then turned to the side to secretly swipe on some lip gloss. "I'll catch up in a minute. If Mrs. Thurber takes attendance, say I stopped in the bathroom, okay?"

Before I could answer, Dana was history. Or rather, I was the one stuck with that.

I found an empty cubby in the library, then slowly read through the handout. You had to make up a question or thesis about some historical event, then support it with evidence from primary sources and write no less than twenty pages—typed up, of course. And did I mention the footnotes and bibliography?

Just reading the assignment made me space out. I reached into my knapsack for my history notebook and pulled out my new sketchbook instead. My friends had been really sweet to give me such a great gift, I thought. I hadn't been very sweet in return. But what they don't know won't hurt them, I decided.

I flipped the book open and started to doodle while my mind wandered. Despite what I'd told Dana, I did have a headache from drinking too much and felt groggy, thirsty, and generally out of it.

I glanced down at the sketchbook and found a drawing. A girl with large eyes and long thick hair. Unreal, ethereal looking . . . yet vaguely familiar. Still, I didn't recognize her. Just a face from my imagination. I closed the book, feeling odd.

I gathered up my belongings and put everything

back into my pack. I'd had enough of waiting for Dana. If she could skip this research session, so could I.

I left the cubicle and started toward the exit through the stacks of books, in case Mrs. Thurber was around.

Just as I rounded the first aisle, I spotted Jackson Turner. He was crouched in front of a low shelf, searching for a book, and didn't see me. I darted around him and did a speed walk out of the library.

I glanced over my shoulder. Jackson was standing now, holding a book and watching me. He didn't call out my name or even wave, but I had a feeling he might follow me.

I turned the corner and ducked into the girls' room, figuring he'd never follow me in there. I stood by the door with my back pressed against the wall. I really should have gone out for lacrosse. A little speed walking and I was panting, as if I'd been running sprints. I was in terrible shape.

I thought the room was empty. Then I spotted Philomena Cantos. She stood at a sink, slowly combing her long dark hair. Today it was pushed back with a wide tortoiseshell band. How sweet and nice was *that*?

She put her brush away and glanced at me. "Are you okay? You look like you're running for your life."

I took a deep breath. Okay, I was out of shape. I didn't need her making me feel worse about it. "I'm fine, okay? Not that it's any of your business," I added.

A pretty nasty comeback, I guess. But I was feeling

awful, and this girl had a way of popping up at the most annoying moments. It was really getting under my skin.

I thought she'd get mad at me, or at least show some reaction. Nothing. Not even a sigh or a frown.

She met my gaze, her dark eyes large and luminous in the dim light, and I could see she felt sorry for me. Of all people, probably the geekiest girl in the grade, *she* felt bad for me. That was funny, right?

Philomena walked past and softly touched my arm as she left the room. A wave of warmth swept through my body. It was totally . . . strange. And it was over so quickly, I thought I'd either imagined it or maybe it was some new hangover symptom.

All I knew was, at that very moment, I felt as if I were going to explode into a billion pieces.

I ran into a stall and slammed the door, then covered my face with my hands. I started crying, my body shaking with uncontrollable sobs. I slid down the metal wall and crouched on the floor.

Why did Matt have to die? Why was he gone forever, while Jackson Turner was still walking around, breathing, talking, watching me?

It was absolutely and totally unfair.

The whole universe stank. That was pretty clear. There wasn't any reason to play by rules of right and wrong. If Matt could die the way he did, it didn't really matter, anyway, did it?

My dad came home at the usual time that night, carrying his suitcase from his business trip. I was up in my room and heard Wiley bark a greeting.

"Brenda? Grace? I'm home."

My mother stood in the foyer beside him as I came down the stairs. They both looked up at me, and I froze about halfway to them.

My father has this great smile. It totally lights up his face. Matt had that smile, too; everybody said so. First I saw the smile, which made me feel good. Then it looked as if a giant eraser swooped down and wiped it off. He stared at me, and his cheeks turned red, right up to his ears. The way they did when he got really angry.

He was just about to say something when my mother touched his arm and shook her head.

He didn't like my hair. Well, that was tough. It was *my* hair, and I had a right to do what I wanted to it. If he made even one tiny comment, I would tell him that, too.

I saw him shake his head and take a breath. "Hi, honey. Come on down. Give me a hug."

He held open his arms, and I finally came down the rest of the stairs and stepped into one of his trademark Big Squeezes.

I hugged him back, inhaling his familiar smell—a spicy aftershave and wool sports jacket.

Then he leaned back and looked at me, his expression wistful. Maybe he was thinking of me as a little girl, with long storybook tresses that reached halfway down my back.

Those days are gone, Dad. So much has changed, I wanted to say.

"For goodness' sake, Grace. Did you have to cut it all off?"

"It's just hair, Dad. It will grow back."

"I think she looks adorable. Short hair is really in style now," my mother piped up before he could answer. She picked up my father's suitcase and set it down next to the stairs. "Wash up, everybody. Dinner's ready."

My father patted me on the shoulder. "Sure . . . it's just hair." Then he turned, following my mom into the kitchen with a sigh.

We were soon seated around the kitchen table in our usual spots. I still found it hard when the three of us were together like this, looking over at the blank spot where Matt used to sit.

Sometimes I pretended he was out somewhere, like at a friend's house or studying in the library. That helped. I wondered if my folks ever did that, too, but I didn't have the nerve to ask them.

My mother took one of my hands, my father reached across the table for the other, and then my father said grace. "Thank you, Lord, for bringing me home to the ones I love, for all the blessings we enjoy and the bounty on our table. Especially the roast beef dinner.

My favorite." He grinned at my mom, then looked serious again. "Bless us and keep us safe. Amen."

My dad put some string beans onto his plate and passed the bowl my way. "So, how's school going, Grace? How are your teachers this year?"

Under his typical parent-type questions I could hear that anxious edge he always had with me and Matt whenever he asked about school. My father wanted both of us to go on to good colleges. He'd never had the chance himself, and that missed opportunity still ate at him. Matt and I had heard the story more than a few times.

My dad had the grades and all the right stuff for medical school. Then his father died of a heart attack right after he'd earned his BA in biology, and he had to return home. It was only supposed to be a temporary thing, but he started working in the family business and had to help support his mother and younger brother. Then he'd met my mother and the rest was history.

So instead of becoming a doctor, my dad had ended up running the insurance agency his father had founded, right back in boring old Greenwood, Ohio, the town where he'd grown up.

Now that I was older, I could understand his disappointment. But I still didn't see how his kids' making good grades and going to good colleges could ever really make that up to him.

Now that Matt was gone, there was no one left to share the pressure. I felt like a bug under a microscope as my dad sat there, alternately chewing his roast beef and asking me questions.

"So, you have Mr. Nurdleman for math this year. How are you doing?"

"It was only the second day of school," I reminded him. "It's hard to tell. We're having a test on Friday," I added. "Nurdleman doesn't waste much time."

Why had I let that slip? I wondered. Now my father would be all over me, wanting to know how I did on the test.

"How do you think it's going to be in college? Teachers aren't going to spoon-feed you anymore. Junior year is very important," he went on.

"I'm sure Grace will do fine. She always does." My mom gave him a look. "More potatoes, Dave?"

My dad took the bowl and dropped a spoonful onto his plate. "When did you manage to cook all this, Brenda? Weren't you working today?"

"I left the office early. I thought you'd appreciate a good meal after all that convention food."

"Tell me about it. I must have gone through a whole bottle of Rolaids." His tone was joking. But lately I'd noticed my dad chewing antacids like after-dinner mints.

My mom smiled at him, and for a few minutes we sat and ate quietly. I thought he'd given up on the school topic, but I was wrong.

"We can find a math tutor if you want, Grace. You can't let your average drop. You'll need trig and calculus to do anything in the sciences."

"I'm not really into the sciences, Dad."

"I know you feel that way now. But why limit yourself? You don't know what will catch your interest down the road. Be prepared. You might want to go in a different direction later on."

Art and literature were my favorite subjects, but my dad didn't get it. He'd say, "You can be good at art and math, too, Grace. Look at da Vinci."

He'd been the same with Matt, always talking up being a doctor or a lawyer, when all Matt wanted was to play his music.

I could almost hear the arguments that had erupted between my father and Matt at this very table. I glanced at my mother and thought she was remembering the same thing. She used to let my dad go on about school and good grades and college when Matt was around. But lately she tried to divert him when she could. Maybe the entire subject made her remember too much.

I didn't want to argue with my father about what I was going to be when I grew up. That seemed sort of pointless to me now. You make all these plans and—poof!—game over.

Who knew if I would even make it to next week? The future was just a theory.

"How about the yearbook, Grace?" he asked.

I'd gone through this with my mother last night, but now I had to do it all over again.

"I'm not going to join this year. I'm too busy."

"Aren't you going to join any clubs?" my mother chimed in. "Or go out for lacrosse again? Colleges look at that, too."

Oh, no. Now she was taking his side. I felt a pang and looked at my plate.

"Too much homework. I don't want to let my average drop."

My dad nodded. "Grace is right. Junior year is very important, and she needs to concentrate. The good schools only take the cream of the crop."

The old "cream of the crop" line. I nearly laughed out loud. It was the same pep talk he used to give Matt. I did an eye roll and automatically glanced across the table . . . but there was no one there to share the joke.

My mother changed the subject, asking my father some questions about his convention in Baltimore. I zoned out. The insurance industry never met anyplace cool like L.A. or New York. It was always Hartford or Cleveland or someplace boring.

Finally we were done, and I helped my mother clear the table. My father took Wiley for a walk, and I went upstairs to finish my homework.

I pulled out my trig book and tried to start my assignment. The equations and curved lines swooping over graphs blurred before my eyes.

I turned on my computer and checked my e-mail. There was one from Rebecca about getting together on Friday night. And another from a screen name I didn't recognize. Then I remembered it was Dana's. She'd told me her e-mail address and screen name the other day.

```
Hi, Grace. Pick out a topic for
our project yet? I was just
wondering. Remember, we have to
hand in the thesis by Tuesday. I
can type it out if you tell me
what it is. Please don't forget.

P.S. When I get my car, you can
drive it anytime.
```

Then she put a little smiley face next to her name.

Fat chance you'll ever get to drive her new car, a little voice chided me. *Wash it, maybe. But drive it? Get real, Grace.*

Get lost, I answered.

Dana *might* let me drive her car. Just for fun sometime. I could see myself in a sleek two-seater with the top down. I was working the stick shift, wearing big sunglasses like Lindsay always wore. I looked really cool, my hair whipping around in the breeze.

Okay, so I don't have long hair anymore. But this was a fantasy. I could give myself long hair if I wanted to.

I heard the signal for an instant message, and the window popped open. JackFlash88, Jackson Turner's screen name, appeared.

```
JackFlash88: It's me, Jackson. Are
             you there?
```

I stared at the computer, afraid to touch it.

I wouldn't answer. He'd think I'd left the room. No problem.

Curiosity got the better of me, though, and I quickly reached down to the keyboard.

```
GraceS_Full: Why are you always
             watching me? It's like
             you're stalking me or
             something. It's really
             weird.

JackFlash88: Weird is good. Better
             to be weird than a
             blockhead jock.
```

He'd seen me getting into Dylan's car yesterday. That's why he'd said that.

I wasn't exactly in love with Dylan, but I was definitely in *like* with him, and I wasn't going to let stupid Jackson Turner trash the guy.

The funny thing was, when Jackson had been around all the time, hanging out with Matt, I'd had sort of a crush on him. A pretty big crush, to be totally honest.

But that was long ago, once upon a time. When I still believed in happy endings. I definitely knew better now.

GraceS_Full: Not all jocks are blockheads, Jackson. I think you're just jealous of all the attention they get.

His answer came back quickly.

JackFlash88: Correction: All jocks are blockheads. YOU aren't paying attention.

I had to laugh, in spite of myself.

GraceS_Full: Okay. Are we done now?

JackFlash88: I just want to talk to you. Why is that so hard?

Why was that so hard? How dare he even ask me that question?

GraceS_Full: If you can't guess, I'm not going to tell you. Talk about blockheads...

JackFlash88: I just want to talk about Matt. With someone who knew him the way I did.

There was a break. I thought he was done. Then he added,

JackFlash88: I miss him so much.

So do I. I miss him more than you ever could. You were just his friend. I was his sister. We didn't even have to talk sometimes; we could practically read each other's minds. Now he'll never tease me again about my funny nose or my big feet. He'll never hug me. Or play his guitar for me. I'll never watch him sing in the church choir or play Frisbee with Wiley. He'll never make us BLTs and leave a big mess in the kitchen for me to clean up.

Meanwhile you're alive and well and having a life, Jackson.

No matter how bad you feel inside, you're still breathing. Your heart is still beating. Why should I feel sorry for you for even one millisecond?

Maybe someone else could. But I couldn't.

The day of the accident, Matt and Jackson had been hanging out at my house. It was July and hot outside, boiling hot. I'd just ridden my bike all the way home from town. When I got in, I realized I'd forgotten to buy milk. My mom had reminded me ten times. She was going to freak.

I didn't want to go back out again. Finally Matt jumped in the car with Jackson, and they headed to a convenience store.

Matt never came back.

But Jackson only got knocked unconscious. He survived the crash with barely a scratch. And somehow I could never forgive him for that.

At Matt's funeral Jackson had apologized to my family, tears streaming down his face. He hadn't been the driver, but he apologized for somehow not saving Matt. My parents had consoled him, told him there was nothing to forgive. Logically I knew they were right. But logic didn't have anything to do with the way I felt.

GraceS_Full: Sorry. I can't help you. You ought to talk to a counselor or something.

I typed it quickly. Then, feeling extra mean, I added,

GraceS_Full: Look on the bright side: At least you're alive and CAN talk, right?

There was no reply for a long time. I wondered if he'd left his computer. I was about to go off line when I saw his answer.

JackFlash88: Technically speaking, I guess you're right. One more question for you.

I hesitated.

GraceS_Full: You can ask. Doesn't mean I'll answer.

JackFlash88: Fair enough. Why do you hate me so much?

I was stunned. At least he was honest. I had to give him credit for that. I typed quickly.

GraceS_Full: I don't hate you.

I *didn't* hate him, either. It wasn't exactly like that. I swallowed hard, trying to be as honest as I could.

GraceS_Full: It's just hard to look at you sometimes. Why are you alive and Matt's dead? It doesn't seem fair. Sorry, but that's the truth.

I waited, wondering if he would answer.

He wrote back.

JackFlash88: I know that. I'm sorry sometimes, too, that I lived and he didn't.

I didn't know what to say to that.

GraceS_Full: What happened to the band?

JackFlash88: You're kidding, right? That's really twisted, Grace.

I wrote back.

GraceS_Full: No joke, I just wondered, that's all.

JackFlash88: There is no band. How could there be?

He's really hurt. It finally hit me. He's hurt the way I am.

I felt a sudden, stunning connection with him. It was so . . . unexpected. But just as quickly I shut down the feeling. I didn't want to feel anything for Jackson Turner.

GraceS_Full: Got to go.

JackFlash88: Okay. Me, too.

And that was that. I sat staring at the monitor like a zombie. I was glad the band had broken up. That was the right thing to happen. But it was still sad. Another part of Matt erased, as if it had never been there at all.

Matt had put his heart and soul into that band. It was all he'd lived for his final summer. It was the thing that made him feel the most alive, the most himself, he'd told me one night after a gig. I remember him pacing around the kitchen, just about bouncing off the walls, he was so wired. All he wanted to do was write songs and get up on a stage and play his music.

It was hard to believe that all that energy, all that light, was gone from the world.

I heard the sound for another IM and wondered if Jackson was back again. But the screen name said Spider-Man, and the message read,

SpiderMan: Hi Grace, it's me. Dylan. Are you there?

GraceS_Full: Yes, I'm here. What's up?

SpiderMan: Didn't get to talk to you today in school. Sorry about that.

GraceS_Full: That's okay.

SpiderMan: Want to catch a movie or something this weekend?

I stared at the message, and my heart did a little *ping*. Dylan Sloan had asked me out! Me, Grace Stanley.

GraceS_Full: Sure, that would be great.

I suddenly remembered the date with my friends on Friday night.

GraceS_Full: Is Saturday okay?

SpiderMan: Saturday is good for me. My mom should be home by then. It's been torture with Bride of the Living Dead this week.

I laughed.

GraceS_Full: Gloria does seem pretty scary.

SpiderMan: You should see her in the morning without her makeup.

Then, before I could answer, he added:

SpiderMan: I hear my dad yelling for me. I'd better go downstairs before he strokes out.

GraceS_Full: Okay. Good luck.

I shut down the computer and flopped onto the bed again with my trig book. I can do this, I told myself. It's only math.

But I just didn't get it. Two days into school, and I was already lost.

Then again, how could I be worrying about a dumb test? Dylan Sloan had asked me on a date. We were practically . . . going out with each other. I was dying to call one of my friends. But it was too late. Besides, it was going to be hard to explain how this thing with Dylan had come about. Rebecca and the others just wouldn't get it.

I sighed and turned off my light, feeling suddenly exhausted.

Why was life so complicated? Sometimes I felt like there was so much coming at me all at once: school, my parents, my friends. My sadness over Matt. I felt like a circus act, spinning plates on skinny sticks. One plate would start wobbling, about to fall off, and I would reach for it, making it spin again. Then another plate would look like it was falling, so I'd have to grab that one.

How many plates could you keep going at the same time?

I felt so tired but couldn't sleep. I stared into the darkness. The number changed on my digital clock. This was the time of night I used to pray. My mother had taught us when we were kids, when she came up to tuck us in. She'd say a little prayer with us and teach us how to talk to God, to tell Him all our worries and plans, to ask for His help.

That got to be a habit, talking to God at night in the dark. A dumb habit, I thought now. Childish, too.

When I closed my eyes again, all I heard was a kind of static. Like a bad phone connection, breaking up.

Hey, Matt. Can you hear me? the voice in my mind said. *I'm not doing too good. Everything seems like too much. The house feels empty without you. Mom and Dad don't do anything except go to church and harass me about college, and—guess what?—I'm going to fail trig. You said you would help me. You promised, remember? I'd give anything to wake up tomorrow morning and find you in your room, snoring away through the alarm clock.*

This is the place where my wandering fantasy got darker. What would I give? Would I give up being able to see? To hear? To walk or talk? Would I be willing to have a disfiguring accident? Lose a leg? Get cancer?

I felt something wet and spongy bump my bare shoulder. Wiley's nose. He panted softly as he stood by my bed.

I reached down and stroked his soft head. "It's okay, Wiley. It's okay," I murmured. He sighed and curled into a tight ball next to the bed, my hand still resting on his head.

Wiley used to stay with Matt at night, and for a long time after the accident, he slept in his room on the floor by his bed. Waiting. Even though my mother kept the door to Matt's room closed, Wiley would edge it open with his nose, and she never had the heart to chase him out.

Lately, though, he came in to be with me.

Even he knew by now that this wasn't just a bad dream.

Chapter Four

I WAS LATE FOR SCHOOL again the next morning, mostly because I'd changed my clothes about a zillion times before leaving the house. I needed the perfect outfit for seeing Dylan; I was sure we'd run into each other in the halls. Having him ask me out on a real date gave me this jumpy feeling, as if anything could happen and I had to be ready.

I'd ended up in faded, low-rise jeans with a plum-colored camisole and a black velour hoodie on top.

When I came down to the kitchen, my dad was at the table, eating cereal and reading the newspaper. He usually left earlier, and I hadn't expected an inspection. I grabbed a yogurt from the fridge and leaned against the counter to eat it. Out of his direct line of view, I hoped. He peered at me over the edge of his newspaper.

"Aren't those pants ready for the Goodwill bag, Gracie?"

"Dad, I just got them."

"Really? Maybe they shrank in the wash. They look a little small on you. And the hems are all frayed."

Luckily my mom breezed into the room then, carrying her briefcase and big red travel mug. My mother used to be disgustingly perky in the morning. Matt always said she must have been a flight attendant in a past life. Now she was brisk and efficient but basically cheerless, pushing herself and everyone else to get out and start the day. I missed the perky, cheerful thing more than I ever would have guessed.

"Come on, Grace. We're late." She leaned over and kissed my father on the cheek. "I'm going to be running around today, so call on the cell, okay?"

Then we were out the door, and he didn't have a chance to make me change.

Dana and I had fun in history class, passing notes and my doodled drawings to each other while Mrs. Thurber lectured about yesterday's reading assignment, which I'd forgotten to read. At the end of class, Dana passed me a note that said, *I can borrow Dylan's car at lunch period. Want to come with us to the deli?*

I turned and nodded quickly. Leaving school for lunch. That was cool. *My* friends never did that.

We met in the parking lot at fifth period. Lindsay seemed surprised to see me again but was starting to get used to the idea, I thought. We drove to a nearby deli and ate at the umbrella-covered tables outside.

Dana glanced at her watch as we were finishing up. "It's ten to one, guys. Do we rush back to school or take our time and cut next period?"

“What a question. I can barely get through a full day of school. It’s pure torture.” Lindsay balled up an empty bag of chips and tossed it at the trash pail.

“I’ll cut. I can’t stand chem lab. It’s such a bore.” Morgan took a long sip of her diet soda.

They all looked at me. I shrugged. “Sure, I’ll cut.” I kept my tone light, as if I cut classes all the time. I didn’t, but it felt like a good time to start.

We got back to school with only two periods left, and the rest of the day flew by. I didn’t see Dylan until just before the last period. He was walking down the hall with two other guys, talking about free-throw percentages, but he stopped when he saw me.

“Hey, Grace. What’s up?”

“Nothing much.” I felt shy all of a sudden. He looked even better than the day before, wearing a navy blue shirt that brought out the blue in his eyes.

From the slow smile on his face, I wondered if he could tell that I was checking him out. “We’re on for Saturday night, right?”

I nodded quickly, like a bobble-head doll. “Right.”

“Cool. I’ll call you.”

More bobble-heading. “Okay!”

He laughed and ruffled my hair. “Catch you later.”

Before I could answer, he was swept away in the crowd.

Okay, so we didn't have the heaviest, most intellectual conversations. But I stood in a daze for a minute, watching until he disappeared from view.

Then I turned and headed for my last class, English. Somehow I'd made it through another day of school, almost an entire week, given that we'd started school on Tuesday.

And I still had Nurdleman's Friday math test to look forward to. . . .

Right after dinner my parents both left for another meeting at church about the homeless shelter. I had the excuse of studying for my math test, so my mother didn't bug me about coming along. I guess staying home on my own was better than watching my mom zone out in front of the TV and having my dad morph into the Phantom of the Basement. But I felt lonely once they left. The house felt so empty.

I was tempted to run upstairs to my computer and go online with my friends. But I took out my math book and some sharp pencils and set myself up at the kitchen table. Then I stuck a bag of popcorn into the microwave. I'd just had dinner, but doing math always makes me crave junk food.

I flipped open the textbook and wrote out an equation on a sheet of graph paper. I crunched some popcorn and stared at the numbers awhile.

"This stuff isn't hard, Grace," I coached myself. "Don't make a big thing about it in your head and get a math block or something, okay?"

I already had a math block in my head. Otherwise known as my brain.

Matt had Nurdleman last year. He said Nerd Man staged sneak attacks, picking kids at random to work impossible problems on the board, then totally humiliating them. If Matt, the math genius, had a rough time with Nurdleman, my prognosis wasn't good.

I crunched some more popcorn, then decided what I really needed to get this study session rolling was a nice, cold beer.

I got one out of the fridge, popped it open, and took a long, frosty gulp. As I sat down again and took another swallow, I could feel the jagged edges in my head smoothing out. I stared down at the trig problem again, deciding that the beer was definitely helping me find the tangent of an angle.

Approximately one hour and two beers later, I slammed my textbook closed and cleaned up, stowing the empty cans outside in the recycle bin. I felt pretty good, floating along on a "don't worry, be happy" kind of buzz.

It was just a stupid math test. Even if Mr. Nurdleman acted as if his course were the most important thing in the world, I knew for a fact it wasn't.

"Okay, people, simmer down. Let's get started." Mr. Nurdleman always called the class "people." What else could we be—trained seals?

"Be sure to complete both pages of the test, front and back. I'll be collecting all the scrap paper as well."

He stood at the blackboard, wearing one of his trademark washable suits. It was rumored he had an allergic reaction to natural fibers and could only wear pure polyester. His curly black hair was cut short on the sides and flat on top. Dark, beady eyes, like a bird of prey's, peered out from behind thick lenses with heavy black frames. Those traits alone would have deemed him a bona fide supernerd.

But the most amazing thing about Mr. Nurdleman was his famous unibrow. It was clearly a case for the *Guinness Book of World Records.* I'd been carefully taught that it was wrong to make fun of people, especially of other people's looks. Nobody is perfect, and all that. But Mr. Nurdleman's unibrow was different. It was one of those things you know you shouldn't keep looking at, but you can't help it. Like when someone has multiple lip-piercings or a gold front tooth.

He handed out the tests, and I lined up my supersharp yellow pencils. When the test reached me, I was almost too nervous to read it.

I picked up my pencil and started in. Concepts that had seemed so clear last night during my beer-and-popcorn review session were now foggy and blurred. I felt Mr. Nurdleman watching while I wrote and erased, then wrote again. He knew I was having trouble. It was unnerving.

"Okay, people. Time's up," he finally announced. "Finish up what you can and hand everything in, including your scrap paper."

Scrap paper. I had plenty of that. I could have wallpapered the entire school with it. It was test answers I didn't have enough of. I walked to the front of the room and tossed my test onto the pile on his desk, avoiding his questioning gaze.

Well, that was that. I'd given it my best shot. What can you do?

*F*s happen.

I knew by now that there are worse things in the world than failing a test. Way worse.

I'd been so pumped up for the math test, the rest of the day felt like a downhill slide. I came home on the bus and hung around in my room, listening to music and doing some drawing in my new sketchbook. I worked on a sketch of Dylan from memory. It came out pretty good. I wondered if I should show it to him.

When my mother came home at around five, I'd just gotten out of the shower and was getting dressed to go out with my friends. The phone rang, and I heard her pick it up downstairs. Then she shouted up to me, "Grace, it's for you!"

I grabbed my extension. "I've got it, Mom." I expected

it to be Rebecca, telling me she was done early with her babysitting job.

But the voice that greeted me was deeper, a guy's voice. "Hey, Grace. It's Dylan."

Dylan was calling me out of the blue. I felt a little thrill go through me. "Hi, Dylan. How's it going?"

"Not so good. My mom was supposed to get home from L.A. today, but now she's not coming in until tomorrow night, and we have to, like, hang out with her."

I felt a pit open up in my stomach. He'd changed his mind about our date and was standing me up.

"Oh . . . too bad," I said slowly.

"But I had this idea," he added. "I know it's short notice, but could we, like, go out tonight instead?"

"Tonight?" He wasn't trying to get out of seeing me after all. That was the good news.

The bad news was if I went out with Dylan tonight, I'd have to ditch my friends. Again.

But would I rather hang out with my girlfriends than go out with Dylan?

Was that even a question?

I would be insane not to go out with him. He'd never ask again.

Besides, it was carpe diem. Seize the day. Be here now. All that stuff.

"Sure. I can see you tonight," I said quickly.

"You can? That's great. You know, I've really been looking forward to getting together again."

His voice got low and sexy, making me remember that afternoon in his bedroom.

"Yeah, me, too," I managed to answer.

I still couldn't believe he liked me. I felt like screaming at the top of my lungs or doing a wild dance around my bedroom.

But I tried to keep it together, at least until we got off the phone.

Dylan suggested we catch a movie at the multiplex, then go somewhere to eat. He wanted to see an action flick about an airplane hijacking. Or maybe car thieves? Neither would have been my first choice, but who really cared?

I heard the call-waiting beep and hung up with Dylan to answer it. It was Rebecca. Talk about timing.

"I survived the Delaneys in one piece," she began. "Well, practically. Can I come over?"

"Um . . . there's this problem. Something just came up." I racked my brain for a good excuse. "It's Nana McVeigh. She doesn't feel well. She wants my mother to go to her house right away, and my mom wants me to come with her . . . in case we have to go to the hospital or anything . . ."

Wow, Ms. Kaplanski was right. I really did have a creative streak.

"Oh, that's too bad." Rebecca sounded concerned. "I hope it's nothing serious."

"Yeah, me, too," I said quickly. "She probably just

messed up her blood-pressure pills again. Can you call everyone and tell them? I'm really sorry," I added, trying to sound sincere.

"Sure. No problem," Rebecca said. "I'll call you tomorrow. I hope your grandmother's okay."

"Thanks . . . thanks a lot."

We said good-bye, and I hung up. I felt a little pang about lying, but quickly brushed it off. I only had a half hour to get ready. No spare time to sit around and feel guilty.

I couldn't wear the outfit I'd planned to wear for my friends. I needed something hot enough to drive Dylan wild, yet modest enough to pass parental inspection.

And how was I going to spring this sudden change in my plans on them?

One minute I was going out with my old gang. And the next, a guy they'd never met before would swoop by in his Jeep Wrangler to pick me up.

Not good. Parents cannot process that quickly.

Ever since Matt's accident my folks had a rule about letting me drive around with kids in cars. I hadn't left the house much for the rule to go into effect yet, but if they didn't know the kid who was driving, they would want to meet him or her first.

The last thing I needed was to have my parents interrogate Dylan in the living room for, like, half an hour. He'd think I'd never been out with a guy before.

The only solution was to lie to my parents. Again.

I quickly dialed Dylan back, hoping he didn't think I was totally neurotic for calling him back so soon. I asked if we could meet at the movie. He sounded puzzled but agreed.

I hung up once more and finished tearing apart my closet, leaving a heap of clothes on the bed and another heap on the floor.

I finally ended up in a dark brown tiered skirt, a thick leather belt, and a stretchy, scoop-neck T-shirt. I put some big earrings and extra makeup into my purse, planning to accessorize in the ladies' room. If I looked too dressed up, my mother would get suspicious.

A short denim jacket buttoned to my chin hid the low neckline and dressed down the look. All I had to do was escape the house before my dad got home and started asking too many questions.

Downstairs, I found my mom at the kitchen counter, chopping carrots on a wooden board.

She glanced at me over one shoulder. "I love you in a skirt. You hardly ever wear one."

"I felt like dressing up a little." My voice sounded thin, nearly cracking. It was hardest to lie to my mom for some reason. Maybe because she always believed me.

"Can you take me to the movies? I have to meet my friends in a few minutes."

"I thought they were all meeting here."

"No, we changed the plan. We're going to the movies first, then out for pizza."

She shut off a burner on the stove and wiped her hands on a dish towel. "Okay, just let me get my keys."

We were almost at the multiplex when my mom said, "Do you need a ride later? We can come and pick you up."

"No, that's okay. Rebecca's mom is coming to get us . . . or maybe Sara's. I'm not sure." I kept it vague just in case my mother talked to one of my friends' parents.

"All right. Call on the cell if you need anything," she said as she pulled into the drop-off area. "We might be out for a while. Pastor James asked us over to the parsonage for coffee, but we shouldn't be too late."

"Oh . . ." That meant my parents were going to our minister's house for more grief counseling. I'd thought they were done with that. Not that they seemed recovered or anything. None of us did. But I, for one, had given up on the talking cure long ago. It only made me feel worse.

"Pastor James was asking about you," she added. "It's too bad you can't come with us tonight."

"Maybe the next time," I said quickly. I grabbed my purse and opened the door, eager to get going.

"Twelve o'clock, Grace," my mother said, reminding me of my curfew.

Twelve o'clock. It just burned me. I knew sixth graders who stayed out later than that. But I didn't have time to argue with her.

"I know. Or else I'll turn into a pumpkin, right?"

"Something like that." My mother smiled mildly at me. "At least a butternut squash."

"Right. Thanks for the warning." I shook my head at her corny joke, then shut the door and stepped up onto the curb. "See you."

"Have fun!" she called before she drove away.

I felt another pang of guilt about lying to her. But you had to tell parents what they wanted to hear so they wouldn't worry, and then go your own way. I was starting to see that very clearly.

It wasn't hard to pick Dylan out of the crowd. He was so tall . . . and cute . . . and he looked really great in a stark white shirt and faded jeans that clung to his narrow hips and long legs.

I would have seen any movie in the world with him. It hardly seemed to matter.

The movie he picked was fast-paced, loud, and, at the same time, extremely boring. There was hardly any dialogue or plot, which I guess made it easy for the actors. Vehicles kept exploding, all kinds: planes, helicopters, several ten-wheel trucks, and lots and lots of cars. An entire parking lot of cars must have been sacrificed for this movie.

Dylan was riveted, reeling his head back and smiling at me when a particularly spectacular explosion or car crash came onto the screen. Sometimes he'd squeeze my hand or say, "Oh, man! Did you see that? Awesome!"

He didn't have a clue that I might find watching car

accidents upsetting. I'd take a long breath and stare at the floor awhile until I was sure the crash scene was over.

Once or twice I almost felt like crying. But I fought off the feeling. I didn't want to make a scene in front of Dylan. Finally the movie was over and the lights went up. I took a deep breath. I felt as if I'd been in a food processor for the last two hours.

"That was great, wasn't it?" Dylan beamed at me.

"It was . . . okay."

He laughed at me. "Not exactly a chick-flick, I know." He made a cute, apologetic face that really got me. "Sorry, Grace. Next time you choose."

"Deal." I was glad to hear he already thought there would be a next time. I grabbed my jacket and purse and headed down our row. Dylan followed, one hand resting on my shoulder.

When we got out to the lobby, he slipped an arm around me and pulled me close. It felt good. I could get used to this.

"What do you want to eat? You get to decide, since I picked the movie," he offered.

"Oh . . . I don't care." I didn't want him to think I was the picky, spoiled, complaining type. Like Lindsay, for instance.

"Why don't we just grab a burger at a drive-thru? I don't think I can wait to sit down and order and all that."

He was going to take me to a drive-thru window on our first date? I guess I'd imagined something nicer. At least an upgrade from the school cafeteria. But what did it matter? I wasn't even hungry.

"Sure. Let's get something fast," I said.

He smiled down at me and hugged me a little closer. "You're so cute."

That got me into a good mood again.

He had his arm around my shoulders, and I slipped an arm around his waist. We walked comfortably in step as we headed to the exit, as if we'd been together forever.

"Grace . . . ? What are you doing here?"

It was Rebecca. She was staring at Dylan as if he had two heads.

Andy and Sara stood a little behind her. Sara gasped out loud and covered her mouth with one hand.

I stood stone still, unable to breathe. I just wanted to disappear. Poof. Gonzo. Vanished into thin air.

"Hi . . . Hi, guys . . ." I dropped my arm from Dylan's waist, but he kept his arm around my shoulders.

He smiled at my friends, looking confident that they would be pleased to pieces to meet the Cougars' varsity power forward up close and personal.

"Hey, girls. You're friends with Grace, right?"

Sara didn't even look at him. She tugged Andy by the sleeve. "Come on. Let's get out of here."

Andy didn't budge. "How's your grandmother, Grace? I guess she didn't have to go to the hospital after all."

"Hey . . . Wait, you guys . . ." I called out to them, though I had no idea what to say.

Sara and Andy turned their backs on me and started walking. Rebecca stood perfectly still. She looked like she was about to cry and didn't want me to see. Then she turned and walked quickly to catch up with the others.

I watched them for a minute, feeling as if a big part of me had been chopped off and was floating away. But it didn't surprise me. I'd seen this coming. I'd known it would happen sooner or later.

Dylan's handsome face crinkled into a frown. "What was that all about? Those girls are, like . . . totally crazy."

"We had some plans for tonight. I switched things around to go out with you and made this dumb excuse so I wouldn't hurt their feelings. I guess they're mad at me for ditching them."

"Weird." He shook his head. "I mean, so what? Get a life, right?"

He didn't get it at all. I'd lied to my very best friends in the world and they'd caught me. They were fed up. They'd never forgive for me this.

I tried to shake off the bad feelings and focus on having a good time with Dylan. I'd have plenty of time to sort things out in my head later. I didn't want him to think I was a total drag.

We got into Dylan's car and headed out to the turnpike, talking mostly about the movie and school. Dylan pulled the Jeep into the drive-thru lane at Burger Haven and asked what I wanted to order. I didn't have much of an appetite but ordered a chicken sandwich and a diet soda.

He quickly gulped down a double burger with cheese, fries, and all the trimmings and then started collecting the trash. He reached for mine before he noticed I hadn't made a dent in my food.

"Are you one of those girls who won't eat?"

I shook my head. "Not usually. I'm just not hungry tonight, I guess."

He nodded but didn't ask more.

We didn't talk much. That was okay with me. He was blasting the music so loudly, we would have had to shout. I wasn't sure where we were headed when he turned off the main road. It wasn't the way back to my neighborhood.

"It's a great night. I thought we could drive up to the Point and get some air," he said.

"As long I'm home by twelve. My parents are really strict about that."

"Twelve o'clock? That's your curfew?" He stared at me, as if to say, *What a baby.*

I flushed and turned to look out the window. "They have their reasons."

He drove faster, and I could tell he was pissed off that I had to be home so early. We made it to the Point in record time. We were the only car there. It was still early for the Point's nightly parking scene.

The Point is a road with big houses on one side and a bluff on the other that looks out over the lake. It's always been a prime spot for parking and making out, and though the cops try to keep kids away, their patrols never really stop anyone.

I'd never been to the Point with a guy before. But I'd never done a lot of things. Dylan seemed to know exactly what he was doing, steering his Jeep into a spot with a perfect view of the lake. It was a clear night, and the sky was dark blue, almost black, scattered with stars, tiny points of white light. Since Matt had died, whenever I looked at a night sky, I couldn't help but wonder about the big questions, the ones that had no end or beginning. No answers, either. Was Matt out there somewhere in that vast emptiness? Was there even a somewhere out there for him to be?

Dylan turned off the engine. The sudden silence snapped me back to attention. "You're very quiet," he said. "Is everything okay?"

I nodded. "Sure. I'm good."

"I have something that will make you feel even better than good." He reached under the seat. "It will make you feel positively great."

He pulled out a small, flat bottle and screwed off the top. He tilted his head back and took a long pull. Then he poured some into his Burger Haven soda cup.

"Here, give me your soda. I'll top it off for you." He

picked up my diet cola from the cup holder and poured the liquor in. He handed it back to me, smiling.

"What is it?" I asked.

"Rum. Try it. It tastes good."

I'd never had rum before, but I didn't want to seem like an even bigger baby. It was bad enough I had to be home at midnight.

I tilted back my head and took a swallow. It tasted really sweet. I hadn't eaten anything all night but a handful or two of popcorn, and the alcohol went right to my head.

"Good, right?" he asked approvingly.

I nodded. "It's really . . . sweet."

He smiled at me, looking looser and maybe even a little drunk already. "So are you. You're really sweet, Grace."

He put his arm around my shoulders and started kissing me. No slow approach like the last time. He just went straight for it. He was on a tight schedule.

The rum made me feel loose and relaxed, almost dizzy. A part of me seemed to be standing back, watching, hardly able to believe I was making out at the Point with Dylan Sloan. How many girls in my school could say they'd done that?

Well . . . probably more than I wanted to know about.

But I was the one with Dylan tonight, and he really seemed into me. That was enough.

We kissed for a while, and it wasn't long before he had my jacket off and had his hands all over me, under my T-shirt and under my skirt. His kisses felt good, and so did his touch. I liked touching him, too. His body felt so strong. I forgot all about the dumb movie and the embarrassing scene with my friends. I forgot about everything, and maybe that felt best of all.

There was just one minor problem. It was hard to make out with the stick shift between us.

"You're great, Grace. You're really beautiful. I really like you," Dylan whispered against my mouth. He dropped his head into the crook of my neck and licked my ear. "Come on, Grace . . . Come on outside with me . . . Let's go out on the grass. I've got a blanket."

I picked my head up and smiled. That seemed like a good idea.

Before I could answer, a beam of light swept across our eyes.

I sat back, quickly untangling myself from Dylan and straightening my clothes. An old man was shining a flashlight into the car. He peered at us through the windshield, then came around to the driver's side and looked in, as if he had a perfect right.

He wasn't a policeman, probably just someone who lived on the street. A little white dog stood up on its hind legs and tried to peer over the edge of the window.

"Hey, you kids. You can't park here. It's no lovers' lane."

"Who the hell—" Dylan began.

"Get moving before I call the cops!" The man waved a cell phone at us.

Dylan started up the car, looking angry enough to explode. "All right. We're going. Keep your pants on, you old fart."

In the light of the flashlight I could see the man's face turning red. "*You* keep your pants on, you little wiseass. Who are you calling an old fart?"

Dylan laughed and pulled out of the space with a screeching sound. My body jerked back in the seat, and I fumbled for the seat belt. He'd had a lot to drink. I hoped the police didn't stop us.

I hoped we didn't have an accident.

Please . . .

I stopped myself, not daring to say the word *God.* Even in my mind.

Please . . . Whatever . . . don't let us have an accident. Okay?

It's not a real prayer, I told myself. *I'm just reaching out to . . . universal energy.*

The whole way home I could feel my heart hammering. It was like being on a roller coaster that had suddenly jumped the tracks. The ride wasn't fun anymore. The ride was going to kill us.

Somehow, though, we reached my street in one piece, only a few minutes past midnight. Dylan pulled into the driveway behind my father's silver compact. The house was dark except for the porch light. It didn't look as if anyone had waited up for me or was peering out a window.

"Here we are. Right on time. That was fun. I mean, until that old guy showed up. What a jerk." He laughed, but I could tell he was still mad.

"Right." I nodded. "Thanks, Dylan. I had a great time."

"Me, too. I'll see you." Dylan leaned over and gave me a hard, quick kiss.

I was relieved that he didn't walk me to the door. After he drove off, I took a moment on the porch to straighten out my clothes and button up my jacket. Then I checked my breath in my cupped hands. Pretty nasty . . .

I popped a few breath mints and unlocked the front door. With the quietest steps possible I started toward the stairs.

"Grace, is that you?" my father called from the basement. I noticed a thin shaft of light shining through the kitchen doorway.

"Yeah, Dad. I'm home. I'm just going up to bed. I'm really beat."

I heard the sound of his steps and waited on the bottom of the staircase, hoping he didn't turn on a big lamp. Or come close enough to smell my breath.

My heart beat wildly in my chest.

"Did you have a good time tonight with your friends?"

I nodded. "Yup. We had fun."

He was staring at me with narrowed eyes. Suspicious . . . or just tired?

"Who dropped you off?"

"Sara's mom," I lied.

"Thank you for coming home on time. We hate to clip your wings, Grace. But we worry." His voice was sad, hinting at a world of painful reasons. "Sometimes it's hard to let you out of our sight at all . . . I don't know what we'll do when it's time for you to go to college."

I didn't know what to say. His words came so slow and thick, I wondered if *he'd* been drinking. No, just crying, I realized.

"How was Pastor James?"

"We had a good visit. A good talk. He's a great help to your mom and me. I don't know if we could have made it without him," he admitted.

Had my parents "made it"? I certainly hadn't.

"Will you come with us next time?" My father took a step closer and put his hand over mine on the banister. "It does help."

I swallowed hard. "I'll think about it."

My dad didn't answer right away. He looked down at his hand covering my own. "Fair enough. You think about it."

I leaned over and gave him a quick, impulsive kiss on the cheek, holding my breath just in case. A risky move.

"Night, Dad. Don't stay up too late."

"Good night, baby."

He always used to say "sweet dreams" to me. Always. But he didn't say that anymore.

Chapter Five

Mr. Nurdleman waited until the end of class on Monday to hand back our tests. He called out our names in alphabetical order, and we walked up, got our papers, and were allowed to leave.

Despite the long wait for the *S*s, I couldn't bear to look at mine right away and waited until I was out in the hallway.

A big, fat red *F* was scrawled on top. Just what I'd expected. Still, I felt my heart sink. I'd never failed a test before. There was a note beside the grade. *See me after class.*

I took a breath and went back into the room. It was empty, and Mr. Nurdleman stood behind his desk, gathering some papers into a file folder.

When he looked up at me, I said, "You asked to see me?"

He nodded and gestured to the chair beside his desk. "Have a seat, Grace. Let's talk."

"I was surprised I failed the test. I really studied . . ." I began.

Okay, so I'd drunk a beer or two. I'd never have been able to sit that long looking at parabolas otherwise.

Mr. Nurdleman's unibrow lowered in a frown. "In a way, that makes this even more serious. If you'd come in here and said, 'Gee, I didn't get a chance to study, and I'll try harder next time,' that would be one thing. But since you studied and did so poorly, that's a concern."

He paused. I looked down at the books in my lap. I felt tears welling up in my eyes but forced them back.

He had a point. I'd tried my best and blown it. And it was only the second week of school. What if I did this badly in all my subjects?

"I know that your family went through a loss this past summer, a truly heartbreaking tragedy. I understand that school probably doesn't seem all that important to you compared with that." He nodded again, his dark eyes surprisingly warm and kind.

"No, it doesn't," I admitted.

"You have a few choices. You can drop this course. There's still time, and it won't show on your record. Give yourself a break. Take it next year or in summer school."

"I can't drop trig. My parents won't let me."

"Okay . . . well, how about some extra help? I could meet with you and go over the test. Or you could get a tutor. I can give your parents some recommendations."

"*Please* don't call my parents." I knew I sounded desperate, but it just slipped out.

Mr. Nurdleman paused, pursing his thin lips. I could tell he was torn, thinking he should call.

"They have enough to worry about right now. I don't want to stress them out."

He sighed. "All right. I won't call. Let's see if we can work this out, okay?"

"Yes. Thanks. I'll come for extra help. I'll do whatever you say," I promised.

"If you can stay after school tomorrow, I'll go over the test with you. And I'll have the names of those tutors."

"Sure, I'll be there. Thanks. Thanks a lot."

I left the room feeling relieved. Nurdleman wasn't nearly as bad as I'd thought. He was a nice guy, and I felt bad for making fun of him.

When lunch period arrived, I discovered a new diet: the avoiding-your-former-best-friends-who-now-hate-your-guts plan. Even though I was starving, I skipped the cafeteria. I figured I could graze at the vending machines later in the day.

All that weekend, after The Great Multiplex Disaster, I kept thinking about calling Rebecca and Sara and Andy. I really meant to. But I never quite got up the nerve. Besides, I wasn't sure what to say, and part of me thought that maybe this was all for the best. They were great people, but maybe I had grown past them. The way they acted, the things they liked to do—it all seemed so boring and childish to me now.

Still, I couldn't bear to face them, so I hid out in the library for lunch. The first phase of the history project was due the next day. I still had some research to do, so I got down to work quickly.

Dana had stopped at my locker that morning to tell me that she wouldn't be able to type up my notes.

"Ellie needed some time off again. To visit her sister in Cleveland or something. She won't be back until Thursday. It's a real pain. Sorry."

"Ellie is your housekeeper, right?" I couldn't make the connection. What did her housekeeper's being away have to do with it?

Dana gave me a look, then nearly burst out laughing. "You didn't really think that *I* was going to type it, did you?"

"Actually, that's exactly what I thought."

Dana shrugged. "So, what are we doing the project on again?"

"The Nineteenth Amendment. Women's right to vote."

"Oh, right. I remember."

"I found a ton of really cool stuff. Lots of letters and all these old newspaper articles and editorials . . ."

"Well, let me have a look sometime. It's my project, too. Remember?"

She'd leaned toward me with a teasing smile. As if I were some geeky project-hog who had totally taken over.

"Hey, jump in anytime, Dana."

"Come on, I didn't mean it that way. Can I help it if you're so much smarter than me? I mean, you're, like, a total brain. How can I compete with that?"

Then she squeezed my arm and smiled again. "It's going to be great. Definite *A*. I have a feeling."

I smiled back, my annoyance at her gone. Okay, so she wasn't into schoolwork. At least she was fun. I could handle the project.

Dana had agreed to meet me in the library during lunch, but I knew she probably wouldn't show. I had been working for about fifteen minutes or so when someone in the cubicle next to me suddenly stuck her head up.

"Hi, Grace. I thought that was you."

Philomena looked like a little prairie dog popping up out of her hole. A smiling prairie dog wearing a pink sweater, her long hair in a single braid down her back. I noticed a little gold cross hanging from her neck, the kind I used to wear. Until I tore it off in a fit and threw it across my bedroom the day of Matt's funeral.

"Oh . . . hi." I looked down at my books again, as if I was really working hard and didn't have time to talk.

Which was not entirely an act.

"How's it going?" she asked brightly.

"Not so great," I admitted. Not that I was about to tell her my life story.

I kept working, thinking she would take a hint. Not Philomena Cantos.

"You didn't join the yearbook after all. Too bad. I saw some of the illustrations you did last year. You're really good."

"Thanks, but I'm too busy this semester." *Hint. Hint.*

"With your boyfriend, you mean? I hope you don't mind my saying this, but Dylan Sloan doesn't seem your type."

"How do you know what my type is? You don't even know me."

She shrugged. "I know enough."

"No, you don't."

"Yes, I do." She nodded slowly, her smile small but certain.

I started to answer, then stopped myself. I wasn't going to sit there and waste time with some silly No-you-don't, Yes-I-do game.

How did she know I was seeing Dylan in the first place? We never hung out around school together. Were people gossiping about us?

Philomena must have read my reaction. She answered my thoughts as if I'd spoken the questions out loud. "I saw you with him at the movies on Friday night. You didn't notice me, I guess."

Had our entire high school been at that multiplex?

Then she gave me this look, and I just knew she had seen the confrontation with my friends. And she felt sorry for me. Again.

"Well, good luck with your project. The suffragettes were really interesting. Good topic idea." She picked up her books and walked off.

How had she known I was working on a project about the suffragettes? I'd never told her that. And I couldn't imagine Dana telling her anything.

Philomena Cantos was just plain weird. She gave off the strangest vibe. All she had to do was look at me, and the hairs on my arm stood up with goose bumps.

I checked out another stack of books from the library, toted them home, and worked all that night on the project thesis.

When I walked into history class Tuesday morning, Dana was perched in the front row, looking cover-model perfect. Her blond hair was fixed in a high ponytail that draped down her back. Her skin glowed, as if she'd been professionally buffed.

Meanwhile, I looked as if I'd been up most of the night and had slept in my clothes. Oh, wait. I had. My hair, what was left of it, stuck up at a funny angle on one side, and when I'd tried plastering it down with gel, it looked even worse.

But the project thesis was done on time, printed out, and ready to hand in. I dropped into the seat next to Dana, and she leaned over to talk to me.

"Sorry I couldn't call you last night. My mom took me to a day spa, and by the time we got back, I was totally beat." She flipped her ponytail over one shoulder and stared at me eagerly. "So, you have our paper ready, right?"

What paper? I was tempted to reply. But I didn't have the energy—or maybe the nerve—to tease her.

"Yeah, it's done. I made a copy for you." I slipped a copy out of my binder and handed it to her. She glanced at it quickly.

"Wow . . . this looks great. You are definitely a total genius, Grace."

"Yeah, right."

I know I am nowhere close to a genius, but compared to the kids Dana usually hung out with, I probably seemed like Einstein.

The period hadn't started yet, and Mrs. Thurber stood in the doorway talking to another teacher.

Dana leaned closer. "Lindsay has her mom's car today. We're going to cruise around after school. Want to come?"

The invitation was definitely a payback. But a juicy one. Lindsay would probably freak if I crashed the party, but I didn't have anything else to do and didn't feel like going home to an empty house. I'd find myself wandering into Matt's room, sitting on his bed. Falling into the black hole again . . .

"Sure," I said. And then I couldn't help asking, "Do you think Lindsay will have a problem with that?"

Dana's smile was smug. "Don't worry, I can handle her. She likes you," she added quickly.

I nodded. "Right."

Dana laughed. "No, I mean it."

Lindsay liked me? She sure had a funny way of showing it. Maybe she'd just told Dana that because she knew Dana liked me. But maybe that also meant I was starting to fit in.

My sketchbook was on my desk, and Dana reached over and flipped it open. "Can I see?" she asked, after the fact.

I usually don't let anyone look at my drawings uninvited, but I didn't want to make a big deal about it. There wasn't too much in there to see, anyway. I still wasn't able to finish a real drawing—only silly little doodles and caricatures. Dana flipped through the first few pages, then came to one I'd sketched on Friday afternoon, hanging out alone in the house.

"Dylan! It's perfect. You've got to show it to him. He'll love it. He'll want to frame it for his room."

"It's okay. I was just messing around." I felt a flush of embarrassment. I'd forgotten about the drawing of Dylan. Now Dana would know I was really into him, and, of course, she'd tell him.

She flipped to another page. The girl with big eyes and long dark hair. That was more of a real portrait, or the start of one. As close as I'd come so far.

"Who's this?" Dana stared at the page.

I shrugged. "Just something out of my head."

"She looks familiar."

The bell rang, and Mrs. Thurber stood by her desk, checking the class roster. I grabbed the sketchbook from Dana and slipped it into my pack.

"Please take out your papers, and I'll collect them."

Before I could pull the paper out of my binder, Dana took the copy I'd given her and waved it the air, right under Mrs. Thurber's nose.

"Here you are, Mrs. Thurber. It was supposed to be double-spaced, right?"

"Yes, that's correct." Mrs. Thurber took the paper and looked it over. "Nineteenth Amendment. Good choice." She looked straight at Dana, not acknowledging me at all.

"Thank you. The research has been really interesting," Dana oozed. "*Lots* of primary sources."

Mrs. Thurber gave Dana another approving look. Before I could get a word in, Mrs. Thurber had moved on.

This day was not starting off so great, but at least I had something to look forward to: cruising around with Dana and her friends.

Lindsay's car, a sleek black convertible, was easy to spot, parked right in the middle of the traffic circle. Lindsay and Dana sat in front, talking and laughing so loudly you could hear them from a mile away. They looked like teen celebrities, ready to shoot a CD cover.

The top was down, and Dana waved to me. Morgan sat in the back, sipping a bottle of water.

I'd had some second thoughts about driving around with them, but I was breaking my parents' rule so often lately, it was getting easier every time.

Just as I headed for the car, I saw Andy and Rebecca leaving the school. They stood by the entrance, and Andy glared at me. She said something to Rebecca, who nodded, her gaze following me.

I quickened my pace, careful not to look back at them.

"Hop in." Dana opened her door, and I slipped into the back.

Lindsay had on her huge sunglasses, as usual. As I settled into my seat, she turned to look at me and pushed the glasses up onto her head.

"Ready for some shopping? We're going to hit the Greenwood Village Shoppes. I bet you go there all the time, right?"

Of course she'd said that to rattle me. Maybe she thought I'd jump out of the car and run away.

I'd been in the Village once, when my mom had to

buy a wedding gift from a bridal registry at a fancy china shop there. The cluster of exclusive stores was built to look like "ye olde faux English village," a far cry from the mall or warehouse-sized outlet stores where I usually went bargain hunting.

"The Village? Sure, I *love* the Village," I said.

Lindsay pushed down her glasses and started the car, throwing back the shift with intimidating ease. "I had a feeling you'd say that."

Lindsay drove at two speeds: very fast and stop. Morgan and I sat pinned against the backseat by wind and velocity.

We soon arrived at the Village and parked. Dana hopped out first and led the way. "Let's go to Outrage. They're having a big sale."

Lindsay trotted quickly to keep pace with Dana, no small feat in her fur-trimmed Ugg boots. "Outrage is the greatest. I hope my credit card doesn't have a meltdown."

"I hope my mother doesn't have a meltdown when she sees the bills."

They laughed, poking each other. I glanced at Morgan, who unwrapped a stick of gum, then broke it in half before chewing a portion.

When we got into the boutique, Dana ran off with Lindsay while Morgan and I went separate ways. I drifted from rack to rack, checking out items here and there, nearly fainting whenever I read the price tags.

About five minutes later Dana came up to me,

carrying an armload of clothing.

"Aren't the clothes here awesome? The owner goes to Europe regularly and buys the absolute latest styles. Didn't you see anything you want to try?"

I'd been caught empty-handed. "Plenty of stuff. I just wanted to look around a little first."

The truth was I *had* seen tons of cool clothes. I was practically salivating. But what was the sense of trying things on when I couldn't even afford a pair of Outrage underwear?

I didn't want to seem like a dweeb with no fashion sense. I grabbed a pair of embroidered jeans and a few tops that had caught my eye and followed Dana to the dressing rooms. It would be fun to try things on. I didn't have to buy anything.

Lindsay was already in a changing room. Morgan stood outside the doors, empty-handed.

"Aren't you going to try anything?" Dana asked her.

Morgan shook her head. She walked to a nearby full-length mirror and began checking out her body. Not that she had much to check. When she stood sideways, you could hardly see her at all.

"I'm so fat, I look like a pregnant whale. It's disgusting . . ."

"Morgan, get real." Dana rolled her eyes and slipped into a dressing room.

"Morgan, you're not fat. Not at all," I said quietly.

She looked at me, then back at her reflection.

"Thanks, but I know you're just saying that . . . I can't try on anything today. I'm too bloated."

I sighed and went into a room next to Dana. Lindsay was the first to emerge.

"What do you think?" I heard her say.

Dana poked her head out of her door and gasped.

"Omigawd! You can't leave without that outfit. It looks *so-o-o* awesome."

I peeked out to see what Lindsay was wearing: a short, pink suede jacket and light gray, wide-legged pants that had a banded sash around the hips. She really did look good.

"Nice jacket. That color is great with your hair."

Lindsay glanced at me. "Thanks." She actually smiled. "Come on out, Grace. Let's see what you've got on."

The outfit I'd picked—superslim-fit jeans covered with all this cool embroidery and a flowered silk camisole edged with lace—was a little over the top. I wasn't really sure I wanted to model it. But I couldn't back down from her challenge.

A pair of animal-print heels with ankle straps had been kicked under a chair in my dressing room, and I slipped them on for maximum effect.

"Grace, we're waiting . . ." Lindsay called to me in a taunting singsong.

I fluffed out my hair, took a deep breath, and wobbled out the door.

"Oooooh!" Dana squealed. "Go for it, Grace!"

I did a slouchy, sulky stroll, imitating a runway model.

Lindsay stood with her arms crossed over her chest. "Definitely an improvement. You *must* buy those pants. How much are they?"

I already knew but pretended I hadn't looked at the tag yet.

"Let's see . . . three-fifty. Hmmm . . . not bad." I struggled for a casual tone as I announced this sum. No wonder they called the place Outrage.

"There's ten percent off today," Dana added helpfully. "So they'd only be about three hundred."

"The pants are . . . okay." I did another turn in front of the mirror.

" 'Okay'? They're perfect for you," Lindsay insisted. "You look really hot. Trust me, I wouldn't say it if it wasn't true."

I did believe her. I knew Lindsay wouldn't say anything just to make me feel good.

"They do wonders for your butt," Dana added decisively.

"Thanks. I think I'm going to try my other stuff."

I slunk back into my dressing room and checked myself out in the mirror again.

I did look good. I looked positively great. I'd never looked this good in my life. It was really . . . me. The new me. I had to buy these pants. I just had to.

So what if the price was outrageous? It was only money.

I kicked off the shoes and dropped onto the charming silk settee. I chewed my cuticles, which I hardly ever do, trying to figure out where this "only money" was going to come from. I had about five dollars and change in my purse, including the linty coins at the bottom.

Suddenly I remembered. . . . The emergency charge card!

I'd been brainwashed so thoroughly by my parents about why and when it could be used—for instance, say I was stranded on Mars and needed to make a collect call—that I'd totally forgotten about it.

I grabbed my purse, flipped open my wallet, and stuck a finger into the tiny pocket under the plastic ID window.

It was still there.

I pulled out the plastic card and practically kissed it. I had no qualms about using it. This was definitely an emergency—a shopping emergency.

I had a momentary vision of my parents when they got the bill, but I brushed the image aside. I'd talk my way out of it somehow.

Something else had been stuck into the hidden pocket and had fallen out with the card. I picked up the scrap of paper off the plush pink rug. I thought it was a receipt or a business card. Then I turned it over.

It was a small square picture of me and Matt. The kind you take in a photo booth at the mall.

We were hamming it up for the camera, Matt with an arm around my neck, practically choking me. My face was right in the camera, with this big cheesy smile.

I let out a long breath, tears pressing behind my eyes.

I could hear him talking in my head, telling me I was acting like a complete idiot.

What are you doing this for? Who are those girls? You don't have to prove anything to them. And those shoes are sad. You look like you morphed into Vanna White.

Very funny. Just . . . can it, okay? I shouted back at him in my mind. *Whoever said you had any taste in clothes, huh?*

Dana's voice snapped me out of my daydream. "Grace, are you ready? We're going to the register."

"Be right out!"

I tucked the photo into a safe place inside my purse, then quickly pulled off the outfit and put on my own clothes.

I shook my head in frustration. I couldn't worry about it now. I just wanted to shop and look good and have fun. Like the rest of the world, for goodness' sake.

I had to show Dana and her friends I was on their level. I had to buy this stuff.

Did you hear me, Matt? I have to do this. Can't you understand that?

The voice in my head didn't answer. There was only an echoing silence, which made me feel even worse.

I stomped out of the dressing room, my arms full of clothes. I got in line behind Dana and, when it was my turn, whipped out the card, trying to look as if I charged things every day.

Just as the salesclerk was tallying up the sale, Lindsay appeared, waving the animal-print heels.

"Don't forget the shoes." She dropped them onto the counter. "They pull the whole look together."

She watched me, to see if she'd finally gone too far. But I took the shoes. Another two hundred, at least. I took everything. I signed the charge slip with a sweeping hand.

A short time later we were back in the car, pulling out of the lot.

"What's next?" Dana turned to Lindsay. "I'm really hungry. Let's get something to eat."

"Good idea. How about something to drink first?" Lindsay leaned over and reached under the seat. She pulled up a big bottle, like a magician pulling a rabbit out of a hat. I could tell from the packaging that it was champagne.

Dana giggled and grabbed it. "Bad girl, Lindsay. You were holding out on us."

"I was trying to control myself." Lindsay was grinning. "Last time we came to the Village trashed, I went over my credit limit and my parents nearly killed me."

"You know what they say, 'Friends don't let friends shop drunk.' " Dana had peeled off the foil on top of the bottle and worked off the wire. I watched as she pushed up the cork with her fingers, and finally it shot off, right out of the car and across the turnpike.

We all started laughing hysterically, and Lindsay drove even faster, weaving in and out of the lanes.

Dana licked the foam at the top of the bottle, then took a long swallow. "Mmm . . . this is the good stuff. Where did you get it?"

"My parents are having a party this weekend. They have so many boxes of booze in the cellar, they'll never miss it."

"You'd better swipe a few more for us, then." Dana passed her the bottle, and Lindsay drank from it, driving with only one hand. The car swerved and I cringed.

Dana passed the bottle back to me. It was heavy and slippery, and I took it in two hands. I lifted it to my mouth. I'd never had champagne before. It tasted like bitter ginger ale. But the others were acting as if it was a real treat, so I did, too.

"Mmm . . . Here, Morgan. It's really good." I held out the bottle, but she waved me away.

"I can't drink champagne. It's loaded with sugar."

"Most liquor has sugar, Morgan," Lindsay said sharply.

"Vodka doesn't," Dana cut in.

"No, gin has the least," Morgan corrected her. You could tell she'd done the research.

"Okay, then you'll have to find some gin in the cellar,

Lindsay, and bring that tomorrow." Dana took the bottle from me and drank a few more swallows.

We drove for a while longer and finished the bottle. Then Dana opened another.

We flew past the Big & Tasty Diner, and Dana shouted at Lindsay to stop. "Here, here! This is a good place."

"No problem." Lindsay tugged the wheel and cut a screeching U-turn across three lanes of traffic and a double yellow line. I squeezed my eyes shut, my fingernails digging into the leather seat.

Car horns blasted at us, and one woman yelled out her window and gave us the finger.

Dana and Lindsay laughed hysterically. When I finally opened my eyes, we were in the parking lot. Lindsay cruised into a space and shut off the engine.

"Did you see the look on that woman's face?" She imitated the driver we'd almost crashed into.

"I bet she, like, wet her pants." Dana doubled over laughing.

Morgan and I laughed, too. I followed them into the diner, my head spinning from the champagne and my heart pumping from the near miss.

We piled into an empty booth, and Dana bounced on the seat across from me. "Don't you just love diners?" She grinned, looking drunk and giddy. Without waiting for an answer, she opened her big menu.

Lindsay opened her menu and closed it quickly. "I hope they have rice pudding."

"Rice pudding? That is so *wrong.*" Dana's tone was half-shocked, half-mocking.

Morgan had a hand over her mouth, as if someone were threatening to force-feed her. "Gross."

"Big deal. I *really* like it." Lindsay's words were slurred and her head slanted to one side. She was totally drunk.

"You *real-l-l-y* like it?" Dana imitated her, making us all laugh. "Well, knock yourself out. But you'll have to eat your pudding at another table."

"It looks so gross, like baby food," I said.

This started us off in another laughing fit, even louder than the first. Everyone was laughing except Lindsay.

She glared at me.

That's for the shoes. I glared back. *Don't mess with me.*

A waitress walked up to our table. I thought my eyes were playing tricks. Or maybe I was so whacked-out from the champagne, I was hallucinating.

No, it was her, all right. Philomena, in an orange waitress outfit, her pad and pencil tucked into an apron pocket. A big plastic badge on her chest said, ASK ME ABOUT OUR BIG SCOOPS!

"Hi, guys. You sound like you're having a good time." She glanced around the table, greeting us as if we were all best friends.

Dana's mouth actually dropped open. "It's you! The girl with the funny name!"

Lindsay and Morgan started laughing even harder.

Philomena kept smiling at her. "That's me, all right."

"Phil-oh-mena," Lindsay pronounced carefully in her drunken voice. "It rhymes with . . . *farina*!"

"Maybe that's her sister's name," Dana sputtered, hardly able to get the words out.

"I don't have a sister," Philomena answered calmly. She shrugged. "Wish I did, though."

"Too bad." Lindsay frowned with fake sympathy. "If you had a sister, she might let you borrow her clothes."

"No," Dana protested, "I *love* what you're wearing today. Orange polyester really works for you."

"Sort of a woman-behind-bars look." Lindsay snickered.

"Or a road-crew look," Dana countered.

"Or a road*kill* look," Lindsay topped her.

We were laughing even harder when Morgan chimed in. "It's definitely hipper than your regular outfits. Very slenderizing, too." She covered her mouth with one hand, bursting with laughter.

Tears squeezed out from the corners of my eyes. Dana was making a snorting sound she couldn't control, which made us laugh even more.

Everything seemed so funny. Hysterically funny. The bubbles from the champagne bounced around inside my head like tiny pinballs. If champagne made you this happy, well . . . I was going to have to drink it more often, like every day.

An older couple at the next table shot us an outraged stare then called over the hostess to complain.

Philomena calmly took out her order pad and pencil and flipped to a clean page. She glanced at me, catching my gaze. She was still smiling calmly, not looking rattled in the least by our mean remarks. But I thought I saw a flicker of light in her dark gaze. A private message. As if maybe she expected this kind of ranking-out from Dana and company, but she expected better from me?

She was definitely strange.

So why did that simple glance get me so unraveled?

I looked down at the table, and all the happy bubbles in my brain burst in one pop.

". . . and I'll have a turkey BLT," Dana was saying. "Hold the *T* . . . and the *B* . . . and put the bread on the side. The left side. Don't let it touch anything. You'd better bring an extra plate. Rye toast, very dry. But don't burn it. And a large order of fries and a diet cola. Oh, yes, and my little *baby* wants some rice pudding." Dana waved a hand at Lindsay. "Can you bring a booster seat?"

Morgan found this hysterically funny.

Lindsay was fuming. "Just an order of onion rings." Her voice was tight, and she practically threw her menu at Philomena.

Philomena finally looked my way. "A brownie and an iced tea," I said.

"Nothing for me, thanks," Morgan said quickly. "Just some water."

Dana laughed at her. "Make sure it's diet water. We don't want her getting any fatter."

Philomena took this down in her earnest way. Had she actually written *diet water*?

"I'll be back in a minute with your drinks." Philomena tucked the pad into her apron and turned to go.

"Hey, Farina, come back a sec," Dana called, and waved a hand.

Philomena turned and quickly trotted back. "Yes? Do you need something else?"

"I forgot to ask you about your Big Scoops."

Philomena looked puzzled.

"That button on your chest. It says, 'Ask me about our Big Scoops!' " Dana's voice was harsh and taunting.

"They aren't in her bra, that's for sure!" Lindsay shouted, then collapsed with laughter.

Heads turned to stare again.

The remark wiped the smile off Philomena's face. But she still didn't look angry. When she finally answered, her voice sounded like a prerecorded announcement.

"The Big Scoop is our two-scoop sundae with your choice of syrup, free when you order any Big & Tasty sandwich platter."

"That's just fascinating. You can get our drinks now." Dana dismissed her with a curt nod.

I watched Philomena turn and head to another table. The others started laughing again, and I did, too. Though I did feel sort of sorry for her, having to work at this diner and wear that dumb button.

No one paid much attention to Philomena as she ran back and forth to our booth for the rest of the meal. The champagne had worn off, and we didn't feel nearly as clever and funny.

Lindsay and Dana huddled together, strategizing about Dylan's friend Ben Kruger. Recently Lindsay had Ben in her sights and was moving in for the kill. Dana had dated him, and Lindsay didn't mind the pass-along, especially the insider advice.

When the check came, Dana swiped it off the table. "My treat, girls!" she announced.

We tumbled out of the booth, mumbling thank-yous. Dana paid the cashier, and we paraded out into the parking lot.

It wasn't until Lindsay's car pulled onto the turnpike that it hit me: No one had left a tip.

Chapter Six

"GRACE, I'D LIKE TO SPEAK WITH YOU. Out in the corridor, please?"

Mr. Nurdleman stood by the doorway, his arms crossed over his chest.

What now? Didn't he have any other students to pick on?

A switch flipped in my brain. I'd forgotten the appointment we'd made to review the test.

Whoops.

"I'm sorry I missed our appointment, Mr. Nurdleman. But my mother called me during the day. Something came up and—"

My excuses started to pour out in a rush. Mr. Nurdleman held up a hand like a crossing guard.

"I waited for nearly an hour. I gave up my personal time to help you. You could have at least extended me the courtesy of leaving a note in my box or even calling me. I can't imagine what this emergency was."

Prancing around a boutique in leopard-skin stilettos. I was certain he couldn't imagine that.

"Frankly, I don't want to know," he went on. "That's not the point."

I nodded again but didn't answer. Whenever adults say, "That's not the point," you know there's way more coming.

"The point is respect, Grace. Respect for others. Respect for their time. Respect for yourself."

His chin dipped down and his tone deepened. I tried not to stare at the unibrow.

I swallowed hard. "Yes, I understand what you're saying—"

The stop-sign hand signal again. "You said you were willing to do whatever it takes to improve your grade in this course."

"I am," I insisted. "Honest."

"That's not what your behavior tells me. Actions speak louder than words."

My mother always said that. It annoyed me and, at the same time, hit a nerve.

"I know I screwed up. I'm sorry for wasting your time, Mr. Nurdleman, and not showing up yesterday. Please, just give me another chance. I'll do extra homework . . . I'll do anything."

He took a long breath and squared his shoulders. I waited for his answer. The hallway was practically empty now, and the quiet made me even more nervous.

"I wouldn't usually. But under the circumstances . . ."

The circumstances being Matt. And how that had totally screwed me up. Of course, he couldn't say that.

"Thank you. Thank you very much." I nodded and swallowed back a tennis-ball-sized lump.

"I can meet with you on Friday, after ninth period."

Friday? Who in her right mind would hang around school for math help on a Friday afternoon? He was doing this just to torture me, I knew it. I also knew I had to agree—and even sound happy about it.

"Friday is perfect. Thank you very much. I *really* appreciate it."

He nodded, his expression still serious. "Just be there. Maybe you ought to write it down in your Day-Timer or something."

"Yes, I will." If I had a "Day-Timer or something."

We returned to the room just as the bell rang. Mr. Nurdleman started the class by calling on kids to do problems at the board. Hard problems. Luckily he didn't pick me. That would have been too cruel.

At lunchtime I peeked into the cafeteria and looked for Dana and her friends. I'd started to think of yesterday's shopping spree and acting out in the diner as sort of an initiation, a hazing ritual without live bugs.

I didn't see them sitting at their usual table. Maybe they'd left the school grounds for lunch. I did spot my old group, though, and was glad they didn't see me.

Even at a distance they seemed to send out icy blasts that practically knocked me over.

I didn't want to hide out in the library again. That was getting old. I wandered outside to the big lawn in front of the school and sat under a tree.

Jackson was sitting on the wall with a few of his friends. He gave me this long, hard stare, as if deciding whether or not to come over and bother me.

Then a friend started talking to him, and they both went back inside the school. I relaxed a little and took a deep breath.

The weather was still warm, but I felt a touch of autumn in the air. A few leaves on the branches above me had already turned color and now drifted down. Time was passing. Days, weeks, months. My life was now split in two. With Matt and without him.

I pulled a brown paper bag out of my knapsack and a copy of *Hamlet*. I should have finished it by now, but I'd barely started. I could definitely relate to Prince Hamlet's melancholy, though.

Sunlight filtering through the branches above made me warm and drowsy. The tree bark felt scratchy through my T-shirt, but I leaned back on the trunk, anyway. I closed my eyes, the book unopened in my lap.

"Want to buy a pretzel?"

I knew that voice by now.

My eyes opened slowly, and I squinted up at Philomena Cantos.

She stood smiling down at me, toting a plastic laundry basket of hot pretzels. A handwritten sign was taped to the basket: PRETZELS—$1.00 / 3 FOR $2.50.

"I'm sorry. Were you asleep?"

"No . . . of course not . . . I was meditating." I rubbed my eyes and tried to hide a yawn. "How many jobs do you have?"

"It's for the yearbook. We're trying to raise money." She put the basket down and sat on the grass next to me.

I wanted to tell her to go away and leave me alone, but I felt bad about the way we'd teased her yesterday.

"I'll buy a pretzel. Why not?"

"They're not hot. But they're not that bad." She handed me one in a napkin and then took one herself.

We didn't talk for a while, just sat chewing and brushing off the salt.

"What happened to all your friends?" she asked, and I wondered if her usual guileless smile was really as innocent as it seemed.

Did she mean my old friends—Rebecca, Andy, and Sara? Or Dana's group?

I avoided the question entirely. "I needed to catch up on some homework."

"Right . . . I guess that group is pretty distracting."

"They know how to have fun, if that's what you mean." I tore off a piece of pretzel and stuck it into my mouth.

"I can see that."

I sat and chewed for a minute, not knowing what to say. What did this girl know about having fun? Did she ever have a minute of fun in her entire pathetic little life?

Why did I even talk to her?

I stuffed the remains of the pretzel into my lunch bag with the rest of the trash, then stuck my book back into my pack and stood up.

"Well, it's been surreal. As usual. Good luck with your pretzels."

The basket was heaped to the top. I'd probably been her only customer. Then I remembered I'd never paid her.

"Wait a sec." I reached into my pocket and took out a wad of dollar bills. I peeled one off and offered it to her. "For the pretzel."

"Oh, right. Thanks." She stuck it into a coffee can tucked inside the basket.

I stood there with the clump of dollars in my hand. Then I held them out to her. "Here, take the rest. It's not much. We forgot to leave a tip yesterday, remember?"

"That's okay." She hefted the basket to her hip. "No big deal."

I knew she was only saying that. Nobody worked at the Big & Tasty Diner for the love of it. She was just proud.

"No, take it. I mean it. You deserve it."

She shook her head, probably surprised I'd say something nice to her.

"You keep it, Grace." Her words floated back to me as she walked away. "It might come in handy. For clothes shopping or something?"

How did she know this stuff?

It was funny: For such a quiet kid, she always got in the last word.

I came home with a heap of homework and set myself up at the dining room table. It was better not to go upstairs when the house was empty and feel tempted to wander into Matt's room.

But I did give in to the temptation to swipe a beer from the fridge. I needed a boost to help me get started on my homework. I popped it open and drank it down quickly. It tasted so good, I had another. Then I wrapped the cans in a plastic shopping bag and stuck them under some stuff in the recycle bin outside.

I felt way better after that, all the jagged edges in my brain smoothed out. I drank a tall glass of diet cola to wash away the beer taste.

My dad came in, toting bags of groceries in each arm. I still had a bit of a buzz but looked like Miss Studious, surrounded by schoolbooks.

"Hi, honey. Lots of homework tonight?"

"Enough." I took a bag and followed him into the kitchen.

He pulled out a carton of milk and one of orange juice. "How was school today?"

I shrugged. "The usual stuff."

I was tempted to tell him about my run-in with Mr. Nurdleman, but I didn't want to admit I was already in math-land quicksand and sinking fast.

"Where's Mom?" I opened the other bag and took out a bunch of bananas.

"She had a meeting at church. About the homeless project. Didn't she call you?"

"No. She didn't." Duh. Why didn't I think of that?

"Is she coming home for dinner?" I sounded cross and sulky but I couldn't help it.

My dad gave me a look. "She should be home in a few minutes. Why don't you set the table? I'll get the food started."

I went to the cupboard and pulled out the plates. I hated setting the table. I always forgot and took out four of everything. I had to keep reminding myself: three plates, not four. Three knives, forks, napkins, and glasses.

My father put a pot of water onto the stove to boil and took a plastic container out of the freezer. I must have been slamming things around more than I realized.

"Hey, you break it, you buy it, lady." He glanced at me, looking curious but amused.

When I looked straight at him, his expression turned more serious. "Anything happen in school today, Grace? Anything you want to talk about?"

I'm failing math. My old friends hate me. I charged a zillion dollars on the emergency credit card. And if you knew half the stuff I've been up to right under your nose? You'd stroke out, Dad.

"Nothing happened. It was a totally boring day."

I swallowed hard and focused on folding the paper napkins into neat triangles.

I heard the front door open, and Wiley skidded down the stairs, barking wildly.

"Hi, everyone. Sorry I'm late."

"We're back here, Brenda. Dinner's almost ready."

My mom came into the kitchen looking energized. I realized it had been ages since I saw that expression. Lately the look in her hazel eyes was dull and flat. Tonight they held a spark.

She gave us each a kiss, then sat in a kitchen chair, catching her breath.

"What happened at the meeting? Did you set the date for the bandfest?"

The bandfest. They were going through with that idea after all. I hadn't realized it was a done deal. I'd been deliberately ignoring the topic, hoping it would just go away.

"It will be three weeks from this coming Saturday. We thought that was enough time to sell tickets and do publicity. The kids say we can draw a big crowd with all this music."

I let out a long breath. It was hard to hear her talk about rock bands.

"Sounds like it's shaping up." My dad tossed salt into the boiling water, then poured in some pasta.

My mother watched me closely. "Something happened at the meeting. I was going to wait, but I might as well tell you now."

My dad turned from the stove. "What happened, Bren? Was there a problem?"

"No, nothing like that." My mom shook her head, her expression serious but not unhappy.

"Listen. Someone proposed that the concert *and* the shelter be dedicated to Matt. To his memory . . ." She didn't look at either of us when she spoke but stared at a spot on the table. "I didn't know what to say. I couldn't say anything, actually. Everyone was in favor of the idea. They really want to do it. I said I would ask you both, though. To see what you think."

"Wow, that's really something." My dad shook his head, looking overwhelmed. "It's good of them to make the gesture. It's . . . very kind."

He turned and pulled out a hankie from his pocket. My mother was crying a little, too, and brushed away the tears.

"Matt's band is going to get together and play at the

concert," she went on. "The whole thing was really Jackson Turner's idea."

I thought I was going to spontaneously combust.

"I can't believe this! How could you let this happen?"

My parents turned and stared at me.

"Grace . . . this is a wonderful way to honor your brother's memory. What's the problem? I don't understand—" my father began.

"You know how Matt believed in helping others—" my mother cut in.

"Jackson Turner is such a liar! He promised me Matt's band would *never* get together again. They'd *never* perform without Matt—"

"But this is a special situation, honey." My dad tried for a soothing tone. "I think Matt would have liked this idea."

"Ha! That's a laugh. I think he would have hated it! Having everyone up there onstage without him, playing his music? Acting as if it makes no difference whatsoever that he's gone?"

"Of course it makes a difference. That's not—"

"Mom! You're just so . . . dense sometimes. Don't you even get it at all? I can't believe you just sat there and didn't say anything to stop them."

My dad stepped toward me. "Wait just a second, young lady. We know you're upset, but you have no right to lash out at your mother and me like this. We're still a family, Grace. We're still in this together."

"Wrong. We are definitely not in this together." He tried to put an arm around me, but I shook him off. "I think church has warped your minds. That's got to be it. There's no other explanation."

"Grace! What a thing to say!" My mother's face had turned as white as paper.

Meanwhile my father's face was beet red. A very bad sign. "How dare you say such a thing! You apologize right now. To both of us!"

He was shouting at me now, but I wouldn't back down.

"You're *always* at church. Always at meetings. You might as well live there. I'm stuck in this house. All alone. Did you ever stop to think about that? Of course not. You must both be brainwashed or something, like you're in a cult."

"That is going too far, young lady! Way too far!" my father shouted.

My mother touched his arm. "Let her finish, Dave. Let's talk about this." She turned to me, her expression pained. "I never knew any of this, Grace. Why didn't you say something? I didn't know you felt lonely when we went to church."

"Well, think about it, okay? You have another kid, you know. It's pretty obvious. Or it should be."

My dad looked furious at the way I'd answered, but for my mother's sake, I guess, he put a lid on it. He stood there staring at me with this tight, angry look.

"Grace . . . I'm sorry you've been feeling that way," my mother began slowly, choosing her words. "I never realized. Your father and I go to church because it helps us."

She glanced at my dad, cuing him to help her out.

My father cleared his throat. "We get some comfort there, Grace. It's so hard sometimes. You know how hard it is. And when we go to church, we feel part of something bigger. We feel closer to God, I guess."

That was all I had to hear. I went right over the edge.

"God? What's so great about God? That's the *great mystery* for me. I hate God. I hate Him for taking Matt away from us, and you should hate Him, *too.* How can you get any comfort from a God who killed your kid? Did you ever think about that? Sitting in church and praying to God and all that?"

My mother gasped. She put a hand to her throat, her eyes squeezed shut as if someone had just struck her. My father rushed across the room and touched her shoulder. "No, I'm okay. Go to Grace. She's hurting so much."

My father turned to me, looking confused, overwhelmed. The only one still standing at the scene of an accident, not knowing what to do.

"Grace." He held out his hands.

I stepped back and shook my head. I couldn't speak.

I turned and ran up to my room. I slammed the door shut and threw myself onto the bed. Tears I'd been holding back for months poured out in gasping sobs. I beat my mattress with my fists and thrashed my legs.

It felt good to finally unload. I didn't care if it shocked them. Or hurt them, even. After all this time of holding everything in, of putting on a happy face and pressing my feelings down, down, until I was choking on them.

It felt good to explode.

I flopped onto my back and stared at the ceiling. I wished Matt were around. I could almost feel the weight of him sitting on the edge of my bed.

"Real smooth, Grace," he'd say with that half smile of his. "They try, but what can I say? It's so hard to raise parents these days. We have to have patience with them."

Somehow he'd always tease me into a better mood.

I twisted onto my side, facing the wall, remembering.

I thought maybe my parents—probably my mother—would come upstairs and try to talk to me some more. I heard them in the kitchen, the sound of plates and pots scraping around. I smelled dinner cooking, but when my father called me from the bottom of the stairs, I pretended I'd fallen asleep.

And I pretended so well, I actually did.

The phone rang. The room was dark, but I could see the time glowing on my alarm clock. It was a little past nine. I picked up the receiver and heard my father talking to someone.

"I don't think she can come to the phone right now. Who's calling?"

"It's Dylan. Dylan Sloan."

"Dylan?" my father echoed.

I sat up and tucked the receiver closer. "I got it, Dad," I croaked. "It's for me."

My dad let out a long, noisy breath and hung up.

"Hi. Are you okay? You sound funny," Dylan said.

"I was sleeping," I admitted. I leaned over and switched on the lamp on my bedside table.

"Oh. Are you sick or something?"

"No . . . I just felt wiped out. A lot going on around here."

"I hear you. Hey, I looked for you at school today."

That woke me up. I hadn't seen much of Dylan since our date. I was starting to wonder if he still liked me.

"I've been around." *Laying low in the library. No wonder you can't find me.*

"You want to go out on Friday night? A bunch of us are planning to hit the clubs."

Clubs? Wow. I'd never been invited to go club-hopping before. "Don't I need ID?"

"Don't you have any?"

I knew some kids had fake IDs, but I wasn't sure where or how they got hold of them. Then again, my old group of friends never tried to get into dance clubs where we'd be proofed for age.

"Could you get one for me?" I asked quickly.

He laughed. "I guess that means you want to go."

"Absolutely."

"Great. I was hoping you'd be up for it. I didn't want to go without you."

Dylan sounded so excited to go out with me, it made me feel really good.

"So, how's basketball practice going?" I knew this was something he loved to talk about.

"I'm so psyched, I'm jumping out of my skin. I can't wait until the season starts. We're just doing scrimmages with other schools now. But we're creaming them, of course."

I pictured myself in the front row of the bleachers, seated courtside near the team bench while I cheered him on. I was wearing something really fabulous, of course. Everyone would know we were together.

"I can't wait to watch you play."

"I can't wait for us to party after the games. I'd better get off now. I have an essay due tomorrow, and I haven't even read the book yet."

"Know the feeling." Before this year I was such a good student, I wouldn't have identified. But now I did.

After we hung up, I leaned back on my pillows, feeling a bit better about life. Dylan's timing had been perfect.

I knew I hadn't heard the last about the blowout. My parents usually took some time to cool off, but sooner or later they always wanted to talk things through. In fact, I was expecting a knock on my door any minute now.

After the way I'd acted and the things I'd shouted at them, they'd probably ground me for the rest of my life. But I wasn't going to miss this date with Dylan. No doubt about it, I was going. One way or another.

By the time I came downstairs the next morning, my father had already left for work. My mother sat at the kitchen table, leafing through a catalog while she sipped her coffee. In my whole entire life I don't think I'd ever seen her buy a single thing by mail order, but she loves to read the catalogs and actually gets upset if anyone throws one out before she's done with it.

"Morning, Grace." She looked up as I pulled out a box of cereal and poured some into a bowl. "Did you sleep okay?"

"Yup." I shrugged as if I had no idea why she'd ask that question.

"I heard you get up and come downstairs."

"I needed a snack."

"Oh. Well, I'm glad you ate something."

I came to the table with my cereal and stared into the bowl. I tried to chew quietly, but the room was so quiet and still, every bite sounded like an explosion.

"Your father and I had a long talk last night."

I looked up at her. I knew what was coming.

"Some of the things you said, Grace . . . well, it was very hard for us to hear you talk like that."

I swallowed and sat back, my appetite vanishing.

"I got a little . . . well, I got really upset," I admitted. "I guess I sort of lost it. I'm sorry."

I wasn't sorry for telling them my honest feelings. But my mother still looked so hurt that I was sorry for lashing out at her.

"No, wait. Let me just finish," my mother said quickly. "We never realized that you felt so lonely. And abandoned," she added, struggling for the right words. "We feel awful if we hurt you, Grace. After everything we've all gone through, we never meant for that to happen. We love you. You're everything to us. All we have left. You know that, don't you?"

I nodded slowly. I knew I'd started this whole mess, but I didn't want to have this conversation. I didn't want to hear my mother talk this way about me.

She shook her head, still struggling. "We're going to do something about this, Grace. We'll figure it out," she promised.

Did that mean they weren't going to go to church as much? I doubted that.

"I don't understand why you and Dad still go to church, after what happened."

"I know you don't. That's okay. Maybe someday you will."

I sincerely doubted that, but I didn't want to argue with her anymore.

"If you don't want to come to the concert, that's fine. If you want to act as if it isn't even happening, that's fine, too. No one is going to force you to take part, okay?"

She paused, watching my reaction.

"That's fine with me," I said.

"Your dad and I are touched that the church wants to honor your brother's memory this way. But I've told you before, this concert wasn't my idea or my decision. It's not fair of you to blame me, Grace."

I met her glance for a moment, then nodded. I hated the idea of this concert and Matt's band playing his music without him. But it wasn't fair to put it all on my mother.

"You're right; I shouldn't have said that," I acknowledged. "And I don't blame you."

Jackson Turner. That's who I really blamed. It had been his idea in the first place. He was the one getting the band back together.

My mom looked as if she didn't really believe me. She looked like she was worried about me, too.

"I know you don't want to come with us to see Pastor James, but your dad and I think you should have some more counseling. We can't make you do that if you don't want to. But we want you to think about it, okay?"

I nodded, struggling to hang on to my temper again. How could talking help? All the talking in the world wouldn't bring Matt back.

"Grace . . . I'm going to work on the homelessness project and the bandfest. That's what I need to do. I hope you can try to think about this in a different way. Not as something your brother would have hated, but as an event that honors him. Could you just try to see it that way?"

I'd never see it that way. So I didn't answer at all.

I sighed and pushed my bowl away, then looked at my watch. "Mom, I'm going to be so late. Can we talk about this tonight?"

She kept looking at me, her expression serious. Then she just shook her head and gave up. "Okay. We'll talk more later. I'd better get going, too, I guess."

On the drive to school my mom suddenly turned to me. "What are you doing after school? I could come home early and take you shopping. We didn't get you much before school started."

Wow. She did feel guilty. She hardly ever offered to take me shopping. But my spree at the Village had cured me of the shopping urge for a while.

"I'm probably going over to Dana Sloan's house," I said, thinking I'd surely get another invitation. "We're doing a project together in history."

We'd pulled into the school parking lot and got into place at the drop-off line. "You ought to ask her over sometime. I'd like to meet her."

"Okay. Does this mean I'm not grounded?"

She looked undecided, her lips pursed. I noticed tiny creases around the edges of her mouth that made her look older. When had that happened?

"No, you're not grounded." She tilted her head to meet my gaze. "You were wondering about that?"

Her tone was lighter, almost teasing.

"Yeah, a little," I teased her back.

She sighed. "If you feel bad, Grace, please . . . try to talk to us. Don't wait so long. Okay?"

"Okay. I'll try."

"I love you, sweetie," she said.

"I love you, too."

She hugged me again and kissed me on the cheek. Her touch lingered for a moment. Finally she let me go.

Chapter Seven

"So everything's set, right?" Dana didn't even bother to say hello. We'd both gotten to history class early on Friday morning; the room was practically empty. "You brought your clothes and everything?"

"It's all in my locker." Including the animal-print heels. I smiled, feeling cool and smug to have pulled off this scam.

It had taken several phone calls and careful planning, but with Dana's advice I'd figured out the perfect cover story for my date with Dylan.

When my mom had dropped me off that morning, she thought I was going back to the Sloans' after school so that Dana and I could work on our project, go to the movies at night, and then have a sleepover.

I didn't need to worry about how I would hide my sexy new clothes before I left the house, because my parents would never even see me wearing them.

"So you're not nervous or anything, right?" Dana, sounding superior, gave me sort of a Mom look. She'd been going out with fake proof for the last two years. Or at least that's what she'd told me.

"I'm not nervous. I wish it was ninth period already. I can't wait."

"Let's cut out early. What's your last class?"

"English. Kaplanski."

I'd been ducking some classes lately, but so far, I hadn't cut English. Ms. Kaplanski was cool. She probably wouldn't make a big deal out of it.

"Okay, I'll cut," I said.

"Very good. My little girl is growing up. Meet me at the back of the parking lot. If Dylan won't drive us, we'll walk up to the gas station and call a taxi. Let's hit Nail Art. I'm dying for a pedicure."

A pedicure? Why hadn't I thought of that?

"Hey, that sounds perfect."

Dana laughed at me and tossed her long hair. "We need to look gorgeous. It's going to be a wild night."

I knew what she meant. Or I could at least imagine. I couldn't wait to wear my new outfit and dance all night with Dylan.

I did feel a little nervous, too. But nothing bad was going to happen, right?

If anything ever happens to you, your folks will never survive it.

I shook my head, trying to chase away the darker

possibilities. *Nothing's going to happen. I need to have a life, too, you know.*

Besides, they'll just go to church some more. Maybe they'll move right in.

I wasn't going to toe the line of good-girl behavior anymore. That was for sure. But clubbing with Dylan wasn't just crossing the line. It was a quantum leap over it.

Part of me believed I was ready. Another part insisted I didn't have a clue.

As the bell rang for ninth period and the hallway emptied, I stood at my locker and pulled out my backpack and duffel. I glanced into the locker again, making sure I hadn't left anything essential behind.

That's when I felt someone tap my shoulder and nearly jumped out of my skin.

Don't let it be Mr. Nealy, assistant principal, on the prowl, please?

I turned around slowly. It wasn't the assistant principal. But almost as bad.

Philomena smiled at me, her dark eyes wide and questioning. "Hi, Grace. Going home already?"

"Maybe, maybe not. What's it to you?"

She shrugged. "You're out here, grabbing all your stuff, and the ninth-period bell just rang. That's all."

"Right. The bell did ring. So why are *you* still out here?"

"I'm on my way to the auditorium. We're watching a Spanish-language film with some other classes."

"You'd better get going. You don't want to miss the previews."

She laughed at my snide reply, as usual. In a strange way I was starting to admire her. It was as if her ego had a Teflon coating.

Instead of taking the hint and moving on, Philomena leaned against the lockers as if she had all day to chat. She eyed my duffel bag. "So, what are you up to for the weekend? Doing anything fun?"

Now she was getting too nosy. Getting on my nerves, as usual. Did she do this to a lot of people, or was I singled out for special attention for some reason?

"Just hanging out. With some friends. I've got to go now." I grabbed my stuff and slammed the locker door closed. "See you."

She nodded. "Sure. Maybe I'll see around over the weekend. You never know, right?"

I laughed at her. As if Philomena Cantos would ever go club-hopping or do anything I did over the weekend.

"Right. You never know," I called back over one shoulder as I headed off to meet Dana. "See you around."

"Get real," I murmured under my breath. That girl was so out there, she needed medication or something.

I met Dana out in the parking lot exactly as we'd

planned. Ditching school early was a snap. Why hadn't I ever tried it before? A short time later, while the rest of my English class sat dying for the bell to ring, I sat paging through a fashion magazine, my feet dangling in a warm whirlpool bath.

After our manicures and pedicures, we called another cab and went back to Dana's. We ordered a mushroom pizza and washed it down with red wine while we watched TV.

Dana's mother called to say she was going on a date with her karate instructor right after work, so she wasn't going to be home at all that evening.

"Maybe not until tomorrow." Dana's blue eyes widened. "He's younger than her, too. And really hot. I told her if she ever gets bored, I wouldn't mind a pass-along."

I couldn't imagine my mother going on dates and staying out all night. Or teasing her about passing along her boyfriends. Dana lived on another planet entirely. It had seemed a strange place at first, but I was beginning to like it.

We both took long showers and then spent a lot of time fixing our hair and putting on makeup. There was a dressing table in Mrs. Sloan's bedroom with drawers full of makeup, the mirror edged by bright white lights. Dana primped there, while I headed for the enormous bathroom.

I normally didn't wear makeup except for lip gloss and dabs of blemish cover-up. But I knew I had to look older tonight, so I gobbed it on. Of course, my hand slipped with the mascara and I gave myself a big raccoon eye.

I opened the medicine chest, looking for some cold cream, and found enough pill bottles to supply a discount drugstore. I took one out and checked the label. The prescription was made out to Dana's mother. ONE CAPSULE EVERY 12 HOURS. FOR ANXIETY.

The instructions seemed written just for me.

Despite what I'd told Dana, I'd been feeling anxious all day. I took one pill with a sip of wine and put the bottle into my pocket. With all the other bottles in there, Mrs. Sloan would never miss it.

I went into Dana's room, all made-up and dressed in my outfit from Outrage. She gasped out loud and practically did a little dance.

"Wow. You look soooo good! I didn't realize you were such a babe, Grace. Wait until Dylan sees you."

That's what I'd been thinking about all day. I wondered about what was going to happen tonight between me and Dylan. Especially after we got back to the house. I'd never slept with a guy, and I wasn't sure I was ready. I had a feeling Dylan more or less expected it. I mean, here I was, partying all night with him, sleeping at his house, no adults home.

If it gets too heavy, I'll figure something out, I decided. What was the big deal about sex, anyway? Adults made it sound so complicated. A lot of kids I knew were having sex. I didn't know if Dylan was The One, but I wasn't going to wait forever. I couldn't see the point to waiting for anything anymore.

It was nearly nine when Dylan got in from basketball practice. The team had gone to another school for a preseason game, and it had been a long bus ride back. Dana and I were dressed and ready to go.

"Whoa, do you look hot!" Dylan grabbed me and planted a big wet kiss on my mouth. He'd showered after practice, and his hair was slicked back wet. "Come up to my room, okay? We can talk while I change my clothes—"

Something would have happened right there and then if Dana hadn't stepped in. "Sorry, you guys don't have time to mess around. We need to leave in half an hour, Dylan. Everyone's waiting."

He made a face but didn't argue. I guess I could have followed him, but I decided to stay downstairs with Dana.

The pill I'd popped was making me feel a little light-headed and loose. I slumped into a leather armchair and drank another glass of wine.

By the time we'd picked up the others—Lindsay, Ben, and this guy Charlie Brockwell, Dana's latest crush—and reached the club, it was just past ten, and the club was opening up.

There had been plenty of drinking in the car, with beer and bottles of liquor passed around. I'd sat pressed next to Dylan in the front seat, and he kept squeezing my thigh.

I'd been feeling really good all the way over but came down with a case of nerves as we walked to the entrance and got in line. Dylan had slipped me some proof—a driver's license and a college ID—that I'd tucked into my front pocket. I thought it looked totally fake, but he promised it would pass.

A tired-looking guy sat on a stool by the door and checked each kid coming in. He had a gold hoop in one ear and wore his grayish black hair in a long ponytail. His T-shirt had a faded decal from a heavy-metal band, covering a potbelly that hung out over the belt of his jeans.

He looked like a guy who definitely preferred heavy beer, and the thought made me sad. Had Matt ever done this? Stepped out with his buddies to some club, used fake proof? If he had, he'd never told me. But there were probably a few secrets Matt kept to himself, things I'd never know about him now.

Dylan stood close behind me in the line and poked me in the back when it was time to show our proof of age.

I held out the fake ID and the ponytail guy glanced at the plastic cards, then at my face. I was sure he was going to laugh and tell me to go home. Then where would I be?

I blinked at him, and he laughed. "What are you, stoned already, little girl?"

He grabbed my hand and pressed it with an ink stamper. It was a purple imprint of a skull and crossbones.

Cheerful touch.

Dylan followed, and I felt myself being pushed through the heavy purple velvet curtain. The other side was like another world.

The sound system in the cavernous room was so strong, everything vibrated: The floor, the ceiling, even the air seemed to pulsate.

The place was already packed, though Dylan and Dana kept saying it was still really early. It was so dark, you could hardly see where you were going, and I kept bumping into people. There were masses of kids everywhere, drinking and laughing.

It seemed as if everyone was older than me—and knew what they were doing.

The club was multilayered, with tiers of tables and private spaces filled with velvet couches and cushy chairs. There was a big dance floor on the bottom level in the center of everything. A long bar swooped along one wall, the edges bordered with a glowing purple light.

"Come on, let's get a drink." Dylan pulled me to the bar. He ordered two beers, and we had a few sips, then went out to dance.

I'd never thought of myself as a good dancer, but I

felt really loose and free that night, moving with the music in a new way.

The more I drank, the better I felt. The better I felt, the more I danced . . . and the more I drank.

The anxiety pill had worked, I decided. When Dylan wasn't looking, I slipped another one out of my pocket and popped it into my mouth.

Dylan could hardly keep his hands off me. He kept pulling me close to kiss, his hands sliding up and down my hips, covering my backside.

"Mmm. Like those moves. Keep it coming." He came up behind me and put his arms around my waist, pulling me back against his body.

We kept dancing, song after song. I felt like I was in a trance. I never wanted to stop moving. The dance floor was like a sauna. My camisole was soaked and stuck to my body like glue. Sweat ran down my legs and made my jeans slide even lower. I kept dancing, tossing my head and waving my arms in the air. I felt totally alive. I wanted to do this every night of my life.

I thought it was the pulsating lights at first. Or maybe I'd lost one of my heels. The whole room suddenly tilted sideways like a fun house, and I tipped to the side, too. I tumbled toward Dylan and he caught me just before I hit the floor.

"Whoooa! Don't fall off those shoes, babe," he teased me.

I felt so giddy, all I could do was laugh. Then I

looked up at him and laughed some more. He helped me stand up and put an arm around my waist.

"Let's take a break. I don't want you to burn yourself out. It's not even midnight."

I staggered beside him. I couldn't see straight and thought it had to be the lights. My brain jumped from one thought to the next, like beads of water on a hot griddle.

I grinned up at Dylan. He looked so cute to me one second, and then the next, like a scary stranger. I couldn't quite keep the picture clear in my head.

We grabbed more drinks at the bar. This time I ordered a rum and Coke. The bitter beer taste was bothering me. I craved something cold and sweet.

I reached for my drink and lifted it to my mouth but somehow missed my lips. A stream of cold soda and crushed ice dripped down my shirt and splashed onto Dylan.

"Oooops." I stared down at myself, laughing.

Dylan smiled but didn't laugh. "You need to sit down. Come on."

He tugged my hand again and led me into a private corner where two little couches covered in purple velvet were arranged as if in a living room. In a house where people liked to sit in the dark.

Another couple was tangled on one of the couches, making out. Dylan sat on the other and pulled me down beside him.

"That's better, right?"

I nodded and had a few more sips of my drink. He took the plastic cup out of my hand and put it down on the floor. Then he leaned over and kissed me, his weight pressing me back until I was stretched out on the couch under him.

My camisole was so wet, he could hardly wiggle his hand underneath. "You're so hot, Grace," he whispered against my mouth. I took his head in my hands and kissed him fiercely on the lips. His body felt hard with muscles.

I meant to say something, but the words kept exploding in my brain before I could get them out, like big bubbles that float for a while and then vanish.

Dylan kept kissing me, his mouth moving over my face and neck, all over my body. He tugged down my top and ran his tongue over the edge of my bra.

I didn't know what was happening to me. It seemed as if Dylan had ten hands. Or maybe there was more than one person on top of me. My head was pounding and I couldn't get a breath.

The bitter taste of beer, mixed with the cola and rum, rose up at the back of my throat.

I turned my head to the side and tried to get a breath. "Get up . . . I need to get up . . ." I managed. He had his face buried against my neck, and he didn't move, didn't seem to hear me.

I pushed at his shoulders with my hands. "Dylan . . . get off me. I have to get up."

I shouted into his ear, and he finally lifted his head. He stared down at me, looking puzzled and angry. "What is it? What's the matter with you?"

I wriggled out from under him, nearly falling onto the floor before he finally rolled to the side and gave way.

"I feel . . . sick or something. I have to find a bathroom."

"Okay, okay. Knock yourself out," he practically yelled, waving one arm in a sweeping gesture.

I skidded to the other side of the bar, where I saw a sign for the restrooms. I was staggering in my high heels, one foot slipping out from under me every other step. I finally made it into the bathroom, one hand covering my mouth.

Two girls stood at the mirrors, working on their makeup. Their spandex skirts were so short, they almost might have doubled as hair bands. As I burst through the door, one of them pulled the other aside. "Watch out, she's going to blow."

I threw myself into a booth and dropped, grabbing the bowl. I felt like a character in a sci-fi flick, as if everything in the universe was coming up out of my stomach.

"Ugh! Let me out of here," I heard one girl say. They ran out of the room and slammed the door.

It took a while for my stomach to settle down. I pulled myself up and staggered out to the sink. When I saw what I looked like, I felt sick all over again.

I had washed my face and was trying to wash off my superexpensive silk top and embroidered jeans when I saw Dana standing behind me.

"Omigawd! What happened to you?"

"I got sick."

"*Duh.* You don't smell so good, either." She pinched her nose and backed away. *Total loser,* her look said.

I'd had a chance to show everyone I could handle this scene. And I'd blown it, big-time.

I squeezed more pink soap from the dispenser onto my hand and rubbed it directly onto my top.

Dana rolled her eyes. "This is hopeless. Come on outside. Everyone's waiting for us."

I took a few more swipes at my top and jeans and followed her back into the club. She walked ahead, as if she didn't want anyone to know we were together.

We stepped outside, past the throng of kids lined up to get in. The sudden silence in the parking lot sounded odd; my ears felt stuffed with cotton.

Dylan flashed the car lights, and we got in. He glanced at me but didn't say anything about how trashed I looked.

"Feeling better?"

I nodded, too embarrassed to say more.

My head had cleared a bit. I was coming down fast from my high, and it wasn't a good feeling. I felt as if I was suddenly on the outside and everyone in the car was laughing at me. Even Dylan. He didn't have his arm slung around my shoulders anymore.

Lindsay passed forward a bottle of sweet wine, and I took a sip. I was wary of getting sick again, but I didn't like this feeling. It was scary. I felt like I wanted to jump out of my skin. Beads of sweat broke out on my forehead and upper lip, even though the night air streaming through the windows was chilly.

"Gross. I can't drink this stuff. It tastes like frigging apple juice." Ben Kruger leaned over and tapped Dylan on the shoulder. "Let's get some more beer, man. Look, there's a Fast Mart. Up on the right."

"You got it." Dylan hit the gas and headed for the convenience store. He pulled into the lot and parked right in front.

"I'm going to come. I need some air." I slipped out of the car and chased after him.

"I'll say she does. She needs some room deodorizer!" Lindsay shouted out, making the others laugh at me.

I trudged behind Dylan, holding my head high, acting as if I hadn't heard her. This night kept getting worse.

How could I guess the *worst* part was still to come?

Fast Mart is one of those 24/7 stores that sells everything from motor oil to disposable diapers. It gives off a weird vibe at any hour, but late at night it seems even weirder. Matt used to call it the "Supermarket of the Damned," and the nickname suited the place perfectly.

I pushed through the glass door and stumbled inside. The long fluorescent lights shone down with a harsh glow; their loud humming sounded like a swarm of bees.

The noise seemed inside and outside of my head at the same time, and I couldn't think clearly or even focus my eyes.

I looked around, wondering where Dylan was. Was he trying to ditch me here?

Then it hit me, where I'd ended up. Not far from home. Not far at all.

This was the place Matt had been headed when he drove into a tree on the turnpike instead. He was on his way here for the milk *I* should have picked up but had forgotten. He'd just gotten his license. I begged him to go for me. I said he was a jerk if he didn't. I'd have to ride back here on my bike in the July heat. He jumped into the car with Jackson. I remember how he pulled out of the driveway slowly, making sure he was clear.

But he never got here.

I gazed around, hating the place. The revolting posters for beer and corn chips. The creepy smell. The bags of pork rinds, the boxes of doughnuts and shelves full of cheese in a can. This awful, ugly place. My brother had been coming here? My beautiful brother? This place was too horrible and ugly to exist.

If it hadn't been here, he never would have had an accident. He never would have died the way he did.

I couldn't stand it. I heard this horrible sound, like somebody choking or trying to scream with their teeth gritted.

It was me. And before I knew it, I had grabbed at a big rack of chips and yanked on it until it toppled over. I gasped and yowled and swiped at a row of cans and pushed them to the floor.

I heard the two clerks at the register screaming at me. One was running toward me, yelling. But I didn't stop.

I felt as if I'd somehow left my body. As if I were just watching the whole scene.

The clerks tried to grab me, but I ran down an aisle. I grabbed some bottles, tossing them to the floor. I wanted to rip this place apart with my bare hands. I wanted to tear down the walls and make the ceiling crash in. I wanted to stomp on those long fluorescent lights and break them into bits.

I started screaming again. Cursing everybody and everything. Cursing out God and my parents and Matt. Even myself.

I flung myself at the magazine rack and pulled out glossies and newspapers, ripping them and tossing them to the floor. I was crying and screaming at the same time. I didn't even know what I was saying.

Someone grabbed me from behind, arms like iron bands around my waist, pinning my arms under his.

"Hey, knock it off. Get a grip. For God's sake. What the hell's the matter with you?"

It was Dylan, holding me and pulling me to the door. I fought him off, kicking at him, but he was stronger.

"You'd better get her out of here, man. What's wrong with her? Is she psycho or something?" The clerk was jumping around us like a jack-in-the-box, waving a fist. "I'm going to get fired for this! We have it all on tape, you know, man. I'm calling the cops!"

"Come on, Grace!" Dylan pushed me out of the store. "Get in the car, damn it!"

He held on to one arm and tried to shove me into the car.

But I twisted out of his grasp and started running.

"Don't touch me! Don't you dare touch me!" I screamed at him.

He ran after me, but I ran faster. I kicked off my shoes and just ran, down the street and around a corner, not looking back once.

I crashed through some bushes and ran behind a row of stores through a dark, empty lot full of Dumpsters.

I came out on the turnpike. I ran onto the side of the road and heard a car honk. It sped by, the wind sucking at me.

I laughed and started walking down the narrow shoulder of the road. It seemed like a good idea. It seemed like the most fun I'd had all night.

If I die out here tonight, I might see Matt again.

That sounded like another good idea.

I felt a stabbing pain in my heart, missing Matt so much it hurt. A blue-black sky studded with stars arched above the roadway. Maybe he wasn't up there at all. Heaven is a hoax, too, a fairy tale. We want to believe in it so we won't be so afraid to die.

There's probably nothing.

You just live for an instant, like the flicker of a match in the dark. Then it goes out and turns to ash. That's it. End of story.

I'm not afraid to die. I was before, but I'm not anymore.

"Hey, God? Can you hear me? I'm not afraid of You!" I shouted to the sky. "I don't even believe in You anymore, so how can I be afraid?"

No answer. Didn't that prove my point?

"If You're up there, why don't You give me some sign, okay? I dare You."

Another car whizzed by, swooping across a lane to avoid me.

"If You're really there, keep the cars from hitting me. I know You think I'm drunk. But I'm not. I swear it. Here, I'll show You. I can walk a straight line . . ."

I ran out to the middle of the road and stopped at the double yellow line. I walked along it with my arms out at my sides, balancing, one foot in front of the other.

Light filled my eyes, blinding me. A car was coming

straight at me. Its horn sounded a long, endless blast, as if the driver was leaning on it. I put my arms up to shield my eyes but otherwise didn't move a muscle.

I squeezed my eyes shut, certain I was going to collide with that glaring white light and die.

The tires squealed, and the car skidded to one side, missing me by mere inches.

I fell to the ground then and just lay there, too terrified to get up.

Headlights came from the other direction, moving slowly. This car cruised to a stop a few yards behind me. The driver's door opened, and someone got out.

Dylan?

No, thank goodness. It was a woman in an orange dress. No, a girl about my age.

"Come on, get up." A hand reached down to me.

I looked up. I couldn't say a word. I had to be imagining this.

"Grace, come on. Take my hand."

It was Philomena, in her waitress outfit. She must have been coming home from the diner. At least she was visible to the oncoming traffic in that getup.

I took her hand and she pulled me off the ground. She tugged me back to her car and opened the passenger door. "Get in."

I considered running again but didn't have the energy. My volcano of anger and craziness had all spilled out of me.

I slipped into the car, and she got in on the driver's side.

I didn't say anything, just stared straight ahead. Then I covered my face with my hands.

"Have a good time tonight?"

"Not really," I admitted.

"Let me know if you're going to be sick again. I like to keep my car clean."

I glanced at her. "Yeah, I can see that. Nice."

It was a VW bug, the original version. Practically an antique, with easily over a hundred thousand miles on it. Not exactly a status mobile, but she seemed proud of it.

Before I could give her the directions to my house, she made the turn off the main road and headed into my neighborhood. "Highland Street, right?"

"That's right," I said quietly. How did she know that?

Philomena pulled up to my house and parked at the curb. "Looks like your parents aren't home. You lucked out."

I was relieved to see the driveway empty. One lucky break for the night. My parents had gone to visit some old friends, a couple who lived more than an hour away. I knew they would be home late, especially since they thought I was sleeping at Dana's house.

I opened the front door, then turned to Philomena, who'd followed me up the walk. "Thanks for the ride."

"No problem. You were right on my way. Well, more like *in* my way."

Her tone was teasing but not mean. She smiled at me in the darkness, her eyes huge and bright. I had that feeling again, like warm honey sliding through my veins. It was so strange and seductive—and scary.

I resisted, shaking it off in my mind.

"Thanks for helping out tonight. Just . . . thanks."

"That's what I'm here for." She shrugged again, the same small but certain smile turning up the corners of her mouth.

Odd answer. Maybe she was one of those religious types with that everybody-is-here-to-help-everyone-else kind of philosophy.

She was freaking me out a little. She seemed to sense that, too.

"It's okay. We can talk another time. You'd better go in before your folks get home."

More good advice. I was so out of it, I'd probably imagined half of this.

I ran inside, then scribbled a note for my parents and left it on the kitchen table.

> *Mom and Dad,*
> *I didn't feel good, so I didn't sleep over at Dana's.*
> *—XXX Grace*

Not entirely untrue, either.

Up in my room I pulled off my outfit and tossed the pile of dirty clothes into a corner. What a waste of money.

Then I took the hottest shower of my life, trying to scrub away the entire night. I pulled on a huge old T-shirt, climbed into bed, and pulled the covers up to my chin. I was so tired, every drop of energy felt drained from my body.

I closed my eyes, and the last image in my head before I blacked out totally was a hand, reaching down to me.

And my hand, reaching up to meet it.

Chapter Eight

When I woke up, bars of bright sunlight had slipped under the shades in my bedroom and the windows made patterns on the blue carpet. I knew it had to be about noon. Or even later.

I remembered my mother coming in to check on me in the middle of the night, and some groggy conversation. Now I smelled coffee and bacon and heard my parents starting Saturday chores.

I pulled on a robe and went downstairs. Wiley sat under the table. He turned to watch me walk in, his tail beating on the floor in greeting. My mother was cleaning the kitchen, wearing yellow rubber gloves.

"Are you okay?" Her voice held a worried note. "I bet you're coming down with something. You don't look so good, Grace." She pulled off a glove and felt my forehead.

"I'm okay. I must have just eaten something funny."

"Do you want breakfast? I saved you some pancakes and bacon."

My stomach ached with hunger, but pancakes and bacon seemed a little ambitious. "I'll just make toast."

I popped two slices of wheat bread into the toaster and poured some juice. My mom started cleaning out the fridge, dumping little plates and containers of left-overs, her Saturday morning ritual.

I started to feel queasy watching her. That's when I knew I had a bona fide hangover. I sipped my juice and picked up a section of the newspaper, flipping to the advice column, hoping to find someone in worse shape than me.

I tried not to ask, but I couldn't help myself. "Did anyone call me?"

She stood up and dropped a rotten piece of fruit into the trash can. "No, nobody called. Why? Were you expecting a call?"

I shook my head and took a crunchy bite of dry toast. "No, I was just wondering."

And I was drawing the obvious conclusion. They didn't even care if I was still alive.

Maybe Dana or Dylan would send me an e-mail. I would check later. I wouldn't be able to stop myself. I'd probably be checking all weekend. I could just imagine Dylan's:

```
Dear Grace--I thought you were cute
and cool. But you turned out to be a
total head case. It's been real....
```

I sighed and rested my chin on my hand. My dad came in the side door. He wore a flannel shirt over a T-shirt and his old khakis, his work-around-the-house outfit. He'd been cleaning up the backyard, and his cheeks looked rosy from the exercise.

"Lots of leaves out there already. I did three bags." Dad always liked to report how many bags he filled. It was important to him. "It's hard to believe. Summer isn't even officially over until next Wednesday."

"Just a cool snap. It might get warm again. You never know with September." My mother sounded as if she wasn't ready for autumn. Neither was I. This past summer had been the most painful season of my life. But I still wasn't ready to let go of it. Not quite yet.

"How are you feeling, Grace?" He patted my shoulder as he passed by. He took a bottle of water from the fridge and poured some into a glass. "Maybe you just needed some extra sleep."

"Yeah, maybe. I feel a lot better this morning."

I didn't feel entirely better, but it had been good to wake up in my own bedroom, in my own house. Something had happened to me last night. Not just the drinking binge and the dance club, or even freaking out at the Fast Mart.

Something had happened to me out on the turnpike. I needed time alone to sort it all out in my head.

After my toast and juice I went back up to my room and booted up my computer.

No message from either Dana or Dylan.

I stared at the message list a second longer, then closed it down. My eyes filled with tears.

I'd been dumped by the MVP of the varsity basketball team, and I was crying about it. Well, I had a perfect right.

But maybe I was crying more because I felt so embarrassed at the way I'd acted. I'd totally lost it, and there was no way I could go back and change that. And I wasn't even sure I wanted to.

The scene had been excruciating . . . but maybe it was something I'd had to go through.

Stupid Dylan. What a conceited jerk. He could barely speak in sentences more than three words long. He could take his MVP trophy and stick it.

I'd never *really* liked him.

I felt a pang. Okay, I'd liked him. I'd liked him a lot.

Even more, I'd liked knowing that he was attracted to me. I had to admit that. I'd gotten off on the status of it. And, for a while at least, he made me forget how badly I was hurting.

As for Dana, I wondered where our friendship stood. Not in a great place, I guessed. Would she still want to be friends with me if Dylan didn't want to see me anymore? Looked as if I'd have to wait until Monday to find out.

Wiley slipped his head under my arm and flipped my

hand off the keyboard with his muzzle. He was carrying a blue Frisbee in his mouth.

"Where did you find that?"

Matt had taught him to play Frisbee, and he loved it. But I hadn't had the heart to take him to the park since the accident. Now there he was, sitting up prettily, holding the disk in his mouth, whining at me.

My parents would be out that afternoon. They were going to buy supplies for the bandfest, then deliver them to the church. I definitely didn't want to go along.

Maybe I could finally handle the Frisbee thing, if Wiley thought he could. Besides, I needed a long walk to clear my head.

When I got to history class Monday morning, the seat next to Dana was filled. She looked my way and waved but didn't say anything.

When class was over, she surprised me by waiting up front so we could walk out together.

"Hi, Grace. How was your weekend?"

What kind of dumb question was that? "Okay, I guess. How was yours?"

"Sort of boring. You know." She shrugged, and her black scoop neck sweater slipped off one shoulder. Definitely cashmere.

I was sure she'd hung out with her other friends and didn't want to tell me.

"That was really wild on Friday night. I thought we were going to have to take you to a hospital or something."

She laughed as if she'd just made a good joke. I cringed.

"Did that ever happen to you before?" She gave me this You-can-tell-me, I'll-understand look, and I wanted to laugh.

"No. It's never happened before. I was just really drunk, in case you didn't notice. That . . . that store we stopped at . . . it was the place . . ."

She stood there, pretending to listen to me, but I could see her eyes glazing over. She kept glancing over my shoulder to see if anyone really cool was passing.

Why am I telling her this? She doesn't care. She doesn't give a damn about me. Or she would have called or come over.

That's what a real friend would have done. What Rebecca, Andy, or Sara would have done. Before I screwed things up with them.

"Forget it. I just freaked out. I guess it was the drinking."

She blinked her eyes, looking at me as if we hardly knew each other. "Maybe you should take it easy, Grace. You don't want to get a real problem."

Whoa. Did I miss something? The Queen of Frozen Margaritas was giving me advice about my drinking problem? My head was spinning.

"Right. Good point." My words came out through gritted teeth. I shifted my books in my arm. "Well, catch you later."

Dana smiled. "Right, see you."

No invitation to hang out at her house after school. I wouldn't be getting any of those again.

I walked off down the hall, feeling as if I didn't have a friend in the world.

Mr. Nurdleman stood outside his classroom like a sentry.

He was *definitely* not my pal anymore.

"Grace, please, I'd like to talk to you," he said before I could go in.

"I'm sorry about Friday, Mr. Nurdleman. I left a note, explaining why I couldn't come to the help session. Didn't you get it?"

He nodded. "I checked with the main office. They didn't have any record of your 'dental appointment,' Grace. And you never signed out in the book on Friday."

I swallowed back a lump in my throat. *Don't worry, Grace. No big deal.* A little voice in my head mimicked Dana.

Of course, I was the one to get caught. What now?

"I guess I forgot to sign out. I really did have to leave early." My words came out in a squeak. I could tell he knew I was lying.

He let out a long, noisy breath. Then he held out a

folded sheet of paper to me. "Let's not get into this again. Here are the names of two good tutors. I'd call right away if I were you. You need the help."

I took the paper and stuck it in my textbook. "Uh, thanks, Mr. Nurdleman."

He looked me right in the eye. "Just do yourself a favor and get on top of this. It's early in the year. You can still catch up."

His words held a tiny spark of encouragement. He wasn't exactly saying I was too dumb to do the work. Just too lazy?

That day in class everyone was asked to pass their weekend's homework to the front, where he collected it for grading. I had forgotten my trig book on Friday in my rush to cut school, and I hadn't done the assignment. So I was back to square one. Or probably on the negative squares by now.

As if the day could get any worse, I was headed for my locker to grab my lunch, when I heard someone calling my name. It was Dylan, standing by his locker. He waved at me, calling me over.

For just a second I felt a wild hope that he was going to tell me that Friday night was no big deal. Everyone gets a little crazy now and then. Bygones.

But I could tell from the look on his face that he wasn't about to say that.

"Hey, Grace. What's up?"

Why did he have to look so gorgeous today on top

of everything? His blue sweater matched his eyes perfectly, and I liked the way he hadn't shaved and his jaw was shadowed with a day or two's growth of beard.

I tried to ignore his looks and focus on how he hadn't even called on Saturday to see if I was okay. "Not much. I'm alive."

"So I noticed." He smiled nervously, then shook his head. "That was some scene on Friday night. Wow. You took that place apart. Lucky we got out before the cops came."

I nodded, hugging my books to my chest. "Yeah, lucky."

He stared down at me a minute and then reached into his locker and pulled out my duffel bag. "You left this at our house on Friday. Dana asked me to give it to you." He shut his locker door with a clang. He stared down at me and I waited to hear what he would say next. "Well, got to run. See you around," he said finally.

That was it. Not only had I just been dumped, I was being told that I'd never be asked back to their house. I'd been booted out of the charmed circle for good.

I felt a sharp stab behind my ribs, worse than I'd expected.

"Sure. See you." I nodded quickly, struggling to act as cool as he was. But Dylan didn't hear me. He was already halfway down the hall.

At lunchtime it seemed a good idea to sit outside again and avoid everyone. I opened my sketchbook to the drawing of Dylan, glad now I'd never shown it to him. That would have made his ego even bigger, if that was possible.

I stared down at it a minute, wondering how best to finish it. Funny glasses and a mustache seemed too clichéd. I wanted something original.

I took my pen in hand and doodled, letting my fingers decide. A few minutes later Dylan's handsome image had been transformed into that of a goofy barnyard animal. A jackass, of course, with big floppy ears, buck teeth, a bristly muzzle, and a dopey look in his eyes. For good measure I put a basketball jersey on him and had him holding a trophy.

I took out a sandwich I'd brought from home, feeling a tiny bit better.

Between Dana and Dylan, everyone in school had to know by now how I'd flipped out at the Fast Mart. I winced. It was so humiliating.

But there was nothing I could do about it.

I flipped through the sketchbook, surprised at how it was filling up. I thought about my friends, and the first day of school. That seemed like such a long time ago. I missed them. I missed hanging out in Rebecca's bedroom, gossiping and listening to Sara's endless stories. I missed talking about guys we liked and girls we didn't, and complaining about our parents. I missed acting crazy with them, dancing to loud music. Trying on clothes for one another or having a cookie-dough fight.

They hated me now. We'd never be friends again. It was one more thing I'd lost this year. Only this time it had been my own fault.

I came to the page with the sketch of the dark-haired girl, and I suddenly knew it wasn't a face from my imagination. It was Philomena, with her hair loose, parted in the middle. This wasn't one of my silly cartoons. It was a real drawing, or could be. I worked on it for a few minutes but didn't get far. I wasn't used to serious work anymore and my sketching reeked.

I munched on my sandwich and stared out into space.

Philomena appeared as if my thoughts had conjured her. As she walked closer, I slammed the sketchbook shut. "No pretzels today?"

"I have the day off." She pulled a brown paper bag out of her knapsack. "May I sit here?"

I shrugged. "Sure."

Yes, she was the weirdest girl in school. But she had saved my life. I couldn't very well tell her to go away.

"What were you doing, drawing something?" She glanced at the sketchbook by my side.

I shook my head. "Not really."

"So, what's the damage?" she asked, looking at the bandage on my knee.

"Just a cut on my knee and my hand." I held up my hand to show her my scraped palm. "I'm not complaining. Considering." I thought about how I'd danced on the double yellow line and then thrown myself down onto the highway Friday night. It seemed like a horrible dream, and I felt a chill remembering.

I looked up, straight into her eyes. "You saved my life. I don't think I can ever thank you enough."

Philomena shook her head. "You didn't want to die, Grace. Not really. I was there to help you—in the right place at the right time."

My first impulse was to argue with her, but her words hit a nerve. I'd thought about it all weekend, and now I finally knew. That was exactly what had happened to me on Friday night. Drunk out of my skull and tempting fate to turn me into roadkill, at the very last minute I'd pulled back from the edge. I didn't want to die, after all. I wanted to live.

"How do you know this stuff?" I was trying not to get spooked, telling myself there was a reasonable explanation.

She took a sip of her iced tea and grinned at me. "Really, you mean it?"

"Yeah." I nodded. "Really. I want to know. It's like you're reading my mind. It's just . . . creepy."

She picked some crust off her sandwich, then popped another bite into her mouth. "I don't know if I can tell you yet. You won't believe me."

Now I was really hooked. "Try me, okay. Just try?"

She looked at me a minute, seeming doubtful. "I'm here to help you. Does that make any sense?"

"That's what you told me the other night. You mean like some universal karma thing: We're all on Earth to help one another?"

Her mouth twisted into a small, wry smile. "Not quite . . . But you're getting warmer."

"Hey, I'm not going to play twenty questions. Either tell me or don't."

"You're the one who asked."

She didn't look upset, just mildly amused at my frustration.

"Well, I don't need any more help. Thanks very much. You've already given me more than enough."

"We're not done yet. Not by a long shot." She shook her head as if I didn't have the vaguest clue about what was really going on.

What *was* really going on? Would somebody please tell me?

Maybe there was no mystery to it at all. She'd been driving home from her job at the diner and happened to see me in the road. So she stopped, maybe just so she wouldn't run me over. What was I working up in my mind? That she had superpowers or something?

Maybe she was completely crazy, or on drugs. That's why she seemed so peaceful—as if she were floating around in a happy cloud.

Philomena crushed the remains of her sandwich into its foil wrapper and pushed it back into her lunch bag. She pulled out an apple and took a big, noisy bite.

She didn't seem in any hurry to argue with me or prove her point.

That got me annoyed, too.

"Look, thanks for stopping when you saw me. Yeah, I needed help. But I'm fine now. I'm just peachy. So let's just let this all go, okay?"

"Okay, you don't need help. You're really fine. That's why you were drinking at Dana's and even stole some pills from the Sloans' medicine chest. Oh, and that's why you talk to a wallet photo of your brother. Because you're so happy and fine."

I cringed. Then I blinked and shook my head. It was like having my own personal spy. Only I knew no one had been spying on me.

"What are you, psychic?"

She laughed at me. "No, I'm not psychic. It's not like that."

Well, what is it like, then? I could have screamed at her. We were talking in circles.

Then she looked at me in that warm, sympathetic way that always got me. "Listen, it's going to take time to get to know each other. It takes time to trust somebody. Do you know what I mean?"

I nodded. That was true. You didn't make friends overnight. Maybe a fake friend like Dana. But not the real thing.

The bell rang, and we both got up and walked toward the building. Philomena smiled to herself, looking as if she'd won this round. Maybe she had.

I still thought she was odd and possibly crazy. But I kind of liked hanging out with her. Our convoluted conversations were growing on me.

It wouldn't be the worst thing in the world to have her as a friend. My friend inventory was getting pretty low. Besides, she seemed to understand things about me that no one else did. And while that was a little unnerving, it was also pretty cool. And it was nice to be around someone who wasn't afraid to mention Matt's name.

When I left school that afternoon, I spotted Dylan sitting in his car in the traffic circle. Some girl ran up to the car and jumped in. It was Brianna Whittaker, a girl Dana enjoyed dissing but acted friendly toward face-to-face.

They drove off, chatting away, Dylan's arm slung around her shoulders. Didn't take him long.

That night at dinner I sensed something was up with my parents. We sat together at the table, and they asked all the usual questions but seemed tense underneath.

When I finished eating, I started to get up and clear as usual. But my mother looked at me and touched my hand. "Sit down a minute, Grace. We need to talk to you."

I glanced at my dad. He looked grim. My stomach dropped, as if I were standing in an elevator that abruptly skipped down a few floors.

My mind raced with horrible possibilities.

They'd gotten the charge card bill.

They'd found the pills in the pocket of my jeans. Had I forgotten to throw them out?

Someone had called—Gloria maybe—and told them I'd been drinking at Dana's house. Or had gone out with fake ID Friday night. Or the Fast Mart had sent them a videotape of my memorable moments.

There were so many things I'd done wrong lately. So many rules I'd broken. So many secrets that would have made them hysterically upset.

"I can't do this now," I said, practically breaking down into tears before either of them said a single word.

"Grace, please. We just want to talk to you," my mother said. "Why are you getting so upset?"

My dad glanced at my mother, his expression serious. They looked like two newscasters about to report a disaster.

I blew my nose on a paper napkin, terrified of what might come next.

"Your guidance counselor called," my father began. "A few of your teachers are concerned about you."

"My teachers?" I took a long breath. Of all the possibilities, that was by no means the worst. I wasn't sure who the others might be, but Mr. Nurdleman was probably leading the pack.

"The school thought we should talk to you first, Grace. They want you to do well, honey," my mother assured me. "This is not a . . . a punitive thing. We're trying to help you."

"We're worried about your average. About college applications," my father said. "Why didn't you tell us you were failing trigonometry?"

My mouth got as dry as sandpaper. "I'm not failing."

"Mr. Nurdleman thinks you are." My father stared at me. "He used those exact words."

"It's only the third week of school. How could I be failing?"

"He said you failed a test last week, and when he scheduled extra-help sessions with you, twice you didn't show up for the appointments. Is that true, Grace?" My mother's tone was milder than my dad's, but she still meant business.

"I . . . I just didn't want to go. Something about him scares me." That wasn't the whole truth but not a total lie, either.

My father gave my mother another one of his serious glances.

"Your English teacher said you didn't show up for her class on Friday. Mr. Nurdleman said you left him a note that you had to leave school for a dentist appointment." My mother shook her head. I could tell it was hard for her to confront me like this. "I don't know, Grace . . . We trust you. We don't like being lied to. That's not the way we raised you."

"You cut out of school early. Just admit it." My dad's voice was getting louder, his jaw jutting out as he continued to question me. "Now, where were you last Friday afternoon? We know you weren't in school."

I swallowed hard. "I did leave school early. With Dana Sloan. I've never done it before, honest." I looked at each of them, hoping they'd believe me. "We went into town and had manicures. Then we went back to her house and ordered a pizza . . ."

That all sounded so innocent. Such girlish fun. Not at all what they'd been imagining. Could they really be angry at that itinerary?

Especially if you compared it to what I'd really done. Washed the pizza down with wine and beer and pills. Then driven around drinking with a bunch of kids and club-hopping with fake ID. And topping it all off with the freak-out in the Fast Mart.

I took a deep breath, wishing I could come clean with them. What a relief that would be. But I knew I couldn't. That just wasn't an option.

"That was it. Honest." I put on my most innocent face.

"You had your nails done. And had a pizza. That's all?" My father repeated the words like a TV cop interviewing a suspect. I could tell he wanted to believe me but didn't entirely.

I nodded slowly.

"Dave, I think she's telling the truth. Let's be reasonable." My mother rested a hand on my father's arm to calm him down.

My father's face was getting redder and redder. My mother didn't look quite as angry. More hurt and disappointed, which made me feel even worse.

My dad took a long breath, and when he spoke, his voice was unnaturally calm. "Okay, you cut out of school early. This one and only time. I guess I can buy that. But that doesn't explain the bad grades." He gave up on the calm and started shouting. "What's going on, Grace? Talk to us!"

That was probably the worst approach to take with me. As soon as someone orders me to talk, I immediately shut down.

I groaned with frustration and leaned forward, my head drooping so that I was looking straight down at the table.

"Grace! Don't look down at the table that way when I'm talking to you! I want an answer!"

I slowly lifted my head, but I still didn't answer him.

And then he got to it. "I received a statement today on the Visa card, Grace. The one we gave you for emergencies only. Did you charge five hundred and eighty-seven dollars at a store called Outrage?"

The credit card bill! I'd been watching the mail every day, but I must have missed it.

A sharp, stabbing pain sliced through my chest. For a moment I couldn't catch my breath. I thought I was having a heart attack.

Before I could say anything, my mother gripped my father's wrist. "Dave, do we have to talk about that now? I thought we agreed . . ."

He spun around and yelled at her, too. "Might as well get it all out on the table. This kid is out of control." He turned and stared at me again. "What the hell is going on here, Grace? Did you use that card to go on a shopping spree?"

I nodded. "I know I wasn't supposed to. But I saw these great clothes and everything was on sale and I thought it would be okay if I used it just that once and paid you back."

"Pay us back? With what?"

"I have money. I have a bank account!" I said indignantly. I did have a bank account with several thousand dollars in it, money from birthday gifts and other occasions. I wasn't allowed to spend it, though.

"That money is for college, not running amok in a mall. What in the world did you buy for five hundred dollars, anyway?"

This was the really hard part. I took another breath. "Some jeans, a top, and a pair of shoes."

My father stared at me, dumbstruck. "Five hundred dollars? For three pieces of clothing? What in the world has come over you? Have you lost your mind?"

I jumped out of my seat, as furious as he was. "Big deal!" I yelled back at him. "What if the jeans were a thousand dollars? Would that really matter? Does stuff like that matter at all? For God's sake, Dad! Don't you get it by now?"

My mother bolted upright in her chair. She looked as if she was about to start crying again. "Stop it, both of you! Just calm down right now!" She turned to my father. "This isn't the way to solve anything."

I wanted to make a run for it, head for my room, and slam the door. But I forced myself to sit down. I leaned back in my chair, my arms crossed over my chest, purposely not looking at either one of them.

My father took a deep breath, then sat down, too. There was a long silence.

My mom was the first to break it. "We know it's hard for you to go back to school this year, Grace. We understand that. But we can't sit back and do nothing while you act out and get yourself into all kinds of trouble. What kind of parents would we be?"

I could tell it was tough for her to admit even that much was happening. The spark of honesty made me finally look up.

My parents both stared at me, hardly breathing.

"It's been hard to be here without Matt. Really . . . hard."

"Of course it's been hard, Grace. It's hard for all of us. We understand, but that's not an excuse to fail your courses and cut school and lie to us and lose all control." My dad wasn't yelling anymore, but his tone was still stern. I guess he was trying to tell me how he was dealing with it, holding it all in so tightly.

But I wasn't like that.

"You don't understand. You just don't." A few tears squeezed out of the corner of my eyes, and I brushed them aside with the backs of my hands.

"Oh, sweetie . . ." My mother's words trailed off. She reached out and took my hand. "We want to help you. Don't shut us out."

How could they help me? They were treading madly and could barely keep their own heads above water. I was getting so tired, I *wanted* to turn to them. But how could I without pulling us all under?

"If you won't talk to us, then please start seeing a counselor again. Please, Grace. We think you have to at least try." My father's voice was quiet but firm.

"How about Dr. Hammer? You liked her, didn't you?" My mother's tone was coaxing, one you'd use to talk to a little kid.

When I didn't answer, my father spoke up again. "Pastor James would see you anytime. He's known you since you were a little girl. He knows our family. Even if you don't want to go with us, you can go on your own. You should give him a chance, Grace."

"Are you going to force me to see a counselor?"

They squinted at each other, thrown by the question. My mother gazed at me and sighed. "No, of course not. You have to want to go. It won't work otherwise."

"We are strongly suggesting you do. We want you to think about this, Grace. Think about it very carefully. Think about your actions and the consequences. I'm afraid for you, Grace. I really am." My dad shook his head, looking upset all over again.

"We know this isn't really you, Grace. It's just not," my mom insisted, as if daring me to contradict her.

We want our little girl back, they might have said. *We don't know this stranger. She scares us. We want everything back the way it used to be.*

So did I, but I couldn't give them back the old me. She was gone. Poof. Vanished. She'd left the scene the very same moment Matt did.

They hadn't figured that out yet, and I wasn't about to start explaining it to them right then and there. They wouldn't listen to me, anyway. They wouldn't believe something they couldn't stand to hear.

"I'll think about what you said. About talking to someone. I will," I promised. "And I'll try harder to keep up with school. I won't cut again. I'm not even friends with Dana anymore," I added. "That was just a . . . a dumb thing."

My dad nodded, and I could see him relax a little. "We don't want you hanging around with her anymore, anyway. So I guess that's one argument we've all been spared."

He hated this, I realized. He hated being angry at me, yelling at me.

"Mr. Nurdleman told me he gave you the names of some math tutors," my mother said. "Give them to me, and I'll call tomorrow." Whenever my mom was upset, she liked to take action, to do something practical to solve the problem. It would make her feel good to call the math tutors.

We all got up from the table and cleaned up the kitchen together. My parents each hugged me and told me how much they loved me. How much they cared about me.

But I was afraid I could never be what they wanted and needed me to be.

I didn't know who to be anymore.

Chapter Nine

WHAT ELSE COULD I DO after that heavy talk with my parents but hit the books? My social life had gone down the drain. There were no distractions with girlfriends—or guys, either, for that matter. I figured, hey, here was my chance to walk on the geeky side. I could live full-time in one of those little cubbies in the library, and nobody would ever miss me.

Nobody except Philomena.

"Studying your lunch away again today? Do you have a test later?"

Her head popped up on the other side of the cubby, startling me. But I was getting used to that.

"No test, just homework. I'm meeting with my new math tutor again this afternoon, and she gave me some problems to work on."

My mother had lost no time scheduling tutoring sessions. It was only Friday, and I'd already met with the tutor twice.

"How's it going? Are you doing any better?" Philomena came around to my side and sat in the seat next to me.

"In a word? No. And I have another trig test on Monday. If I get a bad grade, my folks will flip out."

"Will you?" She seemed curious.

I shrugged. "Right now I'm just trying not to upset them. I might never really care about trig. Or the rest of school."

It was funny how I felt I could be absolutely honest with Philomena. I never felt as if she was judging me.

"Well, give the tutoring some time to sink in," she said finally. "You know, things usually get worse before they get better."

"Get worse? Thanks for the encouragement. I thought you were sent here to help me. Remember?"

We hadn't gone back to our crazy conversation lately, mostly because it always made me feel as if I were going in circles. And what I really needed then was for things in my life to be simple, easy to understand.

Philomena gave me one of her half-sympathetic, half-amused smiles. "Sure, I remember. How could I forget?"

I glanced back down at my trig book. "So, where's the help? Can't you tap me on the head or something and make me a math genius?"

"I don't know. Maybe. But if I could . . . that wouldn't really help you in the long run."

She sounded so serious, she was starting to scare me again.

"Why wouldn't it help?"

"Because it would be trying to turn you into something you're not. And didn't you already figure out that that doesn't work?"

"Do you have to remind me?" I rolled my eyes. "Why do I even get into these conversations with you?"

"Because you like talking with me? I mean, we're friends, right?"

I nodded. I couldn't deny that now. She really was a friend. Partly because she was the only one on my roster lately, but also because Philomena really got me. And while it was a little unnerving to have someone understand me that well, it was also kind of nice.

"People always think of miracles as this sudden thing. Like getting tapped with a magic wand or hit with a bolt of lightning. But most miracles take a long time to unfold. Like a rose in full bloom—you know what I mean?"

She was whispering because we were in the library. But her hushed voice had an urgency to it, almost as if she were praying.

The truth was, I wasn't sure what she meant. Miracles weren't something I thought about very much, and I knew I'd never experienced one. In fact, I couldn't think of anyone who had. Miracles, as far as I was concerned, were the stuff of Bible stories, which were probably total mythology anyway.

I was about to explain all this to her when the wildest thing happened.

The sweet, unmistakable scent of roses filled the

library. I straightened up, looking around to see if someone had passed by wearing perfume. The smell was overwhelming, practically choking me.

Philomena looked amused. "What's the matter? Are you all right?"

"Don't you smell it?"

She shook her head. "No, what do you mean?"

Was she teasing me again? She had to smell the roses. It was impossible for her not to.

"Come on. Don't you smell roses? It's, like, all over the place."

She stared at me and shook her head. "No, I don't. But maybe you do."

I sat back and let out a long breath. The scent was fading as quickly as it had come.

"Hey, you look like you need a break," she said gently. "I think you're getting cubicle fever. Let's get out of here for a while, okay?"

For once I didn't argue with her. I gathered up my books, and we walked out of the library and wandered around the school lobby, where kids hung out during free periods. Philomena said she wanted to show me a ceramic pot she'd made in art class that had been put on display.

Before I knew it, we were walking toward the art room, cutting across the common. I felt sick to my stomach. Had she led me this way on purpose?

"Wait. I don't want to be here." I grabbed her sleeve

but she didn't budge. She gave me a look as if she understood. And I knew she did.

"Philomena, come on. I can't do this. I'm not ready."

She didn't say a word. She stepped back and stared over my shoulder. I turned to see who had caught her attention.

Jackson Turner. After the huge blowup with my folks about the bandfest, I knew that sooner or later I would have to confront him. But I hadn't seen him all week.

And here we were, just yards apart. I could hardly breathe, smothered by all the shadow images of Matt that lingered at this particular spot. I almost turned and ran away.

Instead, I stayed. I needed to confront Jackson more than I needed to run. The bandfest was a week from tomorrow. I probably couldn't change anything, but I could try. I walked straight up to him, forgetting all about Philomena.

Jackson was sitting up on the back of a bench, talking with his pals from the band—Matt's old band, The Daily Dose. He didn't notice me coming, and once he saw me, it was too late. A familiar, righteous fury was surging through me and taking hold.

"I know what you did," I began. "You lied to me. You are such a hypocritical piece of—"

"Grace, man, wait a minute." Jackson looked confused. "What's going on? What you are talking about?"

"The bandfest, Jackson. I know it was all your idea. And your idea to get the band back together. After you promised me you wouldn't. *'There is no band. How could there be?'* " I mimicked him. "Liar! I can't even stand to look at you."

Now the other guys were staring at me. But they didn't say anything. How could they? Everyone knew it was true.

Jackson jumped off the bench, coming right into my face.

"Hey, I didn't lie to you. At least I didn't mean to. It was just an idea we had. I wanted to tell you first, but you never let me come near you. Don't you get it? We're doing this for Matt. We're doing it to help your mom."

"Right. Can't you just be honest for one lousy minute in your pathetic little life? You're doing it for the attention, Jackson. You want to get onstage again and have everyone thinking, 'Poor Jackson. He really misses his friend. How sad. Boo-hoo.' "

The look on his face was terrifying. He turned white, a vein throbbing in his neck. His fists clenched and I thought for a moment he was going to haul off and slug me.

But at the same time his eyes got all glassy. What was he going to do, hit me or start crying or both?

When he spoke his voice was eerily calm. "Who the hell do you think you are? You have no right to talk to me that way. I loved Matt. You weren't the only one.

You act like you own his memory or something. Guess what? You don't."

I felt a lump well up in my throat, and I couldn't talk. Someone pulled on my arm. It was Philomena. I tried to shake her off, but her soft touch was irresistible.

"Leave it, Grace. That's enough now," I heard her whisper.

Two of Jackson's friends flanked him, one on each side, and led him back to their bench.

"Hey, forget about her. She's really lost it since her brother died. She's totally crazed," I heard one of his friends say.

I followed Philomena toward the art room, but just before we left the common, I glanced over my shoulder. Jackson was watching me. He still looked angry but hurt and confused, too. Maybe he was even crying. I couldn't tell for sure.

The righteous rage I'd felt was gone, and in its place was a sick, shaky feeling. Another fabulous scene. This was getting to be a habit. What if I really was just a drama queen? But when I thought of Matt's band playing without him, I couldn't be sorry for what I'd just said.

"Are you all right?" Philomena asked.

"Yeah," I said. "I had to get that off my chest. This isn't the end of it with Jackson."

"Not if you don't want it to be." She didn't sound as if she was in my corner. More as if she felt sorry for me.

Whatever. I couldn't change my feelings. I was tired of trying.

I glanced at Philomena. "Don't give me that look," I murmured.

"What look?"

"You know. Like I'm a total screwup but you love me anyway."

She looked straight ahead again, smiling to herself. "Sorry. I can't help that."

I'd been afraid she was going to say something like that.

Still, it made me feel a tiny bit better.

As Philomena had predicted, it did feel sometimes as if things were getting worse. I missed my old friends. I found myself staring at them from across the cafeteria or hallway. They weren't giving me those cold, angry looks anymore. Instead, they didn't acknowledge me at all, which was even worse.

I was sitting on the lawn with Philomena one day when the three of them passed by. She caught me looking at them, even though I pretended I hadn't been.

"You ought to apologize," she said quietly.

"Apologize to whom?"

She ignored my dumb question. "I think they miss you, too. They're just too proud to make the first move."

I shook my head. "They don't miss me. Besides, what would I say?"

Philomena just looked at me. She didn't say anything more. But I guess she'd planted the idea in my head. Because one night, not too much later, having nothing better to do, I wrote an e-mail to them. It was short and to the point.

```
Dear Rebecca, Andy, and Sara--
I don't quite know what to say,
but for a while now I've wanted to
say something. So here goes. I'm
not asking you to be friends with
me anymore. I know by now that
that's hopeless. I totally
understand why you got fed up with
me. I guess I just want you all to
know that I'm sorry I lied to you.
--Grace
```

I wondered if any of them would answer. After a couple of days when no one did, I decided that it was one of those things I wasn't going to let myself think about.

Every day I went straight home after school and studied. I still had an overdue essay in English to make up, and I had to keep up the work on the history project I was supposedly doing with Dana but actually was doing all by myself. Part of me really wished I could have a beer to take the edge off, but the other part got nauseated just thinking about alcohol.

On Tuesday morning Dana officially bailed on me. She caught up with me just outside Mrs. Thurber's room before I walked in. She smiled briefly.

"No offense, Grace, but Mrs. Thurber said it's okay if I team up with Brianna Whittaker. I don't mean to ditch you. But you seem like you want to do our project all by yourself, anyway," she added.

I didn't even ask what their topic was going to be. Probably something like the history of the miniskirt.

You won't get an A *with Brianna. Let's see if your father springs for that new car, Dana.*

"That's fine," I said quickly. I shrugged. "Have fun."

I gave her a totally fake smile and walked into the classroom, heading for a seat in the back row.

I felt stung for a moment, dumped yet again.

But I quickly shook the feeling off. It was actually a relief. At least Dana wouldn't be taking credit for my work.

While I pushed to catch up with my schoolwork, my mother was putting in long hours preparing for the bandfest. She didn't talk about it much in front of me, but I could hear her discussing it with my father when they thought I wasn't listening.

My parents rarely left me alone in the house anymore. Either they didn't trust me or they were afraid I'd be lonely—I was never sure which.

I was spending more time with my dad in the evenings now. He made a real effort not to disappear into the basement, and I made an effort to be sociable.

On Tuesday after dinner he and I took the dog for a walk downtown. He'd already grilled me about school at the dinner table, so we didn't talk much. We walked in the crisp night air through our neighborhood, under the streetlights and the arching branches of very old trees. These trees had seen so many seasons. The approach of winter didn't worry them. Not the way it worried me sometimes.

Strolling down the familiar streets, I could almost pretend that nothing bad had ever happened to my family. I wondered if my dad was pretending that, too.

It's not as if I forgot about Matt for a single instant. I knew I never could. But there could be, for a few moments at least, a kind of peace that carried me a short distance. Before I had to let it go.

"Your mom is working hard," my dad said. "Too hard. I'm worried about her."

"It will be over soon. The bandfest is Saturday. Just a few days left."

He glanced at me. "I didn't think you were keeping such close track."

I didn't say anything. I was waiting for it all to be over—but for my own reasons.

"You haven't changed your mind about coming, I guess?" His tone held a hopeful note.

"No, I haven't."

"That's what I thought. I was just asking." He shrugged and didn't say anything more about it.

The next day Philomena came home with me after school. I felt as if I'd known her so long, it almost seemed odd that she'd never been to my house. There was always some reason she couldn't come: the yearbook, or her job at the diner, or homework.

When we got in, Wiley ran barking to the front door to greet us. He's not the best-trained dog in the world and is usually a pain with visitors, especially someone he hasn't met before.

"You like dogs?" I asked, grabbing his collar to hold him down. "He gets a little wild around strangers."

That was an understatement. Wiley had a funny way of trying to win people over. He didn't realize that most visitors don't appreciate being knocked down and licked until they were unconscious.

"It's okay. You don't have to hold him. I love dogs. He's beautiful. Hello, Wiley."

Philomena tilted her head and smiled. Wiley circled around in front of her, panting a little, but for once he didn't jump up. I let go of his collar and stood back.

I'd never seen Wiley this calm before around a visitor, even someone he knew. Philomena leaned over and held out a hand. He gently pressed his nose to her fingers, then lay down at her feet, staring up at her as if awaiting further commands.

She leaned over and patted his head. "He's so sweet. I love the fur around his ears. It's like little feathers."

I stood there dumbstruck. The dog had never acted

like this before. Never in his life. Maybe I needed to take him to the vet.

"Want to walk down to the park? He really needs to go out." Even though he wasn't showing it, which was also strange. Usually he'd be barking his head off at me by now if I didn't put his leash on as soon as I got home.

It was a short walk to the park, and we followed a narrow path to a pond surrounded by a Japanese garden. I unleashed Wiley and let him go, knowing he wouldn't stray too far.

The Japanese garden wasn't all that much compared to some famous gardens. But it was nicely done and not the usual thing you find in our town. The place had fascinated me and Matt when we were little; sometimes we even asked to go there instead of the playground. We could stand forever at the water's edge, watching the orange and black carp dart around beneath the clear water and lily pads.

"Did you come here with Matt a lot?"

She'd picked up my thoughts again, as if my brain were a radio station and she could tune right in. I wasn't even startled anymore, which was a scary thought in and of itself.

"The last time we came here together was in the spring," I remembered. "It was pretty with all the cherry blossoms."

Matt had been looking forward to the summer, itching for school to end. He had a job stocking the shelves at a big home-improvement store and planned to spend the rest of his time with his band.

"It looks a lot different this time of year." I gazed around. The little garden was still serene, but the autumn leaves were already falling, and it was almost as if I could feel everything going bare and stark for winter.

"I think it's really beautiful." Philomena followed me over the footbridge, and we stood side by side in the middle. "I love the fall."

"I used to . . . but not so much anymore."

We stood there, staring into the water. Neither of us said anything for a long time.

The water was so still, you could see the reflection of sky on its surface, yellow and orange leaves floating across the clouds.

"It was my fault, you know. I don't think I ever told you."

My voice was so quiet, I wondered if she had even heard me.

Then I felt her hand on my arm. "I know you think that. But you're wrong, Grace."

"No, I'm not," I insisted. "I was the one who sent him out. I practically begged him. I was too lazy to go out again. It was so hot, I didn't feel like riding my bike all the way back to the Fast Mart for a stupid container of milk. He didn't want to go, you know. He argued with me. But I talked him into it."

"You did." She nodded, not asking a question but as if she'd been right there and seen it all happening. "But that still doesn't make any difference."

"Of course it does. It makes all the difference. How can I ever forget what I did, sending him out that way?"

"Is that why you're so mad at Jackson Turner?"

"Jackson? What does he have to do with this?

"Well . . . if you stopped blaming yourself for Matt's dying, you'd have to stop blaming Jackson, too. Then there wouldn't be anybody to blame anymore. You'd be stuck."

"No, I wouldn't. I'd still blame God. I already do."

"I thought you didn't believe in God anymore. How can you blame Him if you don't even believe God exists?"

She gave me this innocent, confused look, her dark eyes wide and deep. As if I had stumped her, when I knew it was just the opposite.

"I don't know!" I nearly shouted. "I just do, okay?"

"Okay." She shrugged.

"You know what the last thing he said to me was?" I didn't wait for her to answer. "He said, 'You owe me for this one. Big-time.' "

She nodded. "Yeah, you do. That's true."

I gave her a puzzled look. "Great. So how should I make it up to him? Make his bed? Or do his chores around the house?"

I knew I sounded cutting, and I didn't mean to be. But the whole conversation made me hurt inside again something awful.

"You can start by forgiving yourself. You didn't have control over whether Matt was going to live or die that day. Nobody did. We'll get to the rest later."

I wanted to believe what she said. But I couldn't. I'd been clinging to this guilt so tightly, I couldn't let it go that easily.

"There you go again with this . . . this . . . bizarre way of talking. Do you ever realize how crazy you sound? Sometimes I don't even know why I hang around with you. And don't tell me you were sent here to help me again, okay? That is getting so . . . tired."

"But that's the way it is." Philomena remained as calm as our surroundings. She held a handful of colored leaves and dropped one onto the water, then watched it float away under the bridge. "I think you *are* starting to believe sometimes. You're just not ready to admit it."

"I *don't* believe you. I don't believe you at all!" I yelled. "Who sent you? God? I don't believe in Him, remember?"

"He believes in you." She paused and looked me in the eye. "Big-time."

"Oh, give me a break."

"You can't escape God, Grace, just because you don't go to church. He's everywhere. He's inside and outside of you. His thoughts flow through you. I think you do feel Him here. That's why you like to come here, why you brought me."

"I brought you here because it's *nice,*" I insisted.

She ignored me and kept talking. "He was out in the middle of the turnpike the night I picked you up. And in the bathroom stall at the club, when you puked your guts out—"

"Enough. I get the idea." I turned away from her. My hand gripping the bridge's wooden railing was trembling, and I didn't know if it was from anger or fear. "Why did Matt have to die, then? If you know so much about everything, answer that one for me."

"Oh . . . I can't answer that."

"Perfect. That's exactly what I thought you'd say. I bet if I asked you to tell me where Matt is now, or to show him to me, you couldn't do that, either, right?"

"Why ask *me*? You can see him anytime. You can talk to him. I know you already do. He's listening. He hears you." She turned and faced me.

Philomena wore her hair down, pushed back with a wide band. The breeze lifted up a few strands and blew them over her shoulder.

I'd never realized how pretty she was. Really . . . beautiful. Not like some popular girl with perfect clothes and makeup. But as if there were a light shining way down inside her.

I'd never really seen it before, and now I felt nearly blown away.

"You'll always be connected to Matt. Through your love. That's the most powerful force in the universe. It's like this bridge, connecting both of you through time and space and everything you think of as the real world, Grace. When you feel his spirit near, he is there," she assured me, "watching over you."

I wanted to believe that. I really did. I couldn't deny that sometimes I felt that Matt was close but I couldn't see him or touch him. And I never knew if what I was feeling was a memory of Matt or just another game I played in my head to keep from feeling too awful. But now Philomena was telling me it was real.

"It's all energy, Grace. Nothing is real the way you think it is. Nothing is what it appears to be."

I blinked and shook my head. "How did we start talking about God and end up with a physics lesson?"

"Some people say the study of physics is, at its heart, a search for God. Einstein said that, I think."

I didn't know enough about Einstein to argue with her.

As I walked to the other side of the bridge, she followed. She tossed the rest of the leaves over the water and they scattered in all directions, like confetti, as if we were secretly celebrating something.

I was on the Net looking for essays on the flower symbolism in *Hamlet* when the instant message window popped open. I hardly ever IM'd lately. My old friends weren't speaking to me. No one had answered my e-mail. Dana had dropped me, and Dylan had forgotten I even existed.

There was only Philomena, and she didn't go online much.

JackFlash88 was sending me a message.

Jackson Turner. I was about to turn on my *Away* message, but curiosity got me. I decided to see what he had to say.

JackFlash88: Grace, you there?

GraceS_Full: I'm here.

JackFlash88: I have to tell you something.

He'd probably thought over our confrontation and had some snarky comeback for me. I do that a lot. Run a scene over in my mind and think of the clever things I should have said at the time.

GraceS_Full: Are you going to tell me how horrible I am again?

JackFlash88: It's not about you. Or me, either. It's about Matt.

That got my attention.

GraceS_Full: Go ahead, I'm listening.

JackFlash88: This is what I didn't say to you the other day. But it's the most important thing. The reason I'm doing this is for Matt. So his music can live on. So some small part of him still exists in the world. I know this concert thing hurts you. It hurts me, too. I know you don't believe that. But it does.

I wasn't going to answer. But then . . .

GraceS_Full: I believe you.

And I did.

JackFlash88: So...isn't that important to you? Can't you put your own feelings aside for him? I feel like I owe him that much. I owe him big-time, you know?

His choice of words made my breath catch in my throat. It was just a coincidence. A turn of phrase. Everyone says it.

But it didn't feel like a coincidence.

It felt like a message. A sign. Like that time I smelled the roses. I almost expected to start smelling them again now.

JackFlash88: Grace, are you still there?

GraceS_Full: I'm here.

JackFlash88: That's what I needed to explain to you. But I'll call this whole thing off if you still don't understand. If you still don't want the band to get back together, we won't. It's your call. Totally.

I couldn't believe he was saying that. I couldn't believe that after everything—even the crazy way I'd acted out on him—he'd do that for me.

But there it was, in black and white, right on my screen.

GraceS_Full: How could you? The bandfest is Saturday. That's only three days from now.

JackFlash88: Don't worry. I can get another band for your mom. She'll understand. It will work out, I think.

She would be disappointed, but I also knew she would understand.

I didn't know what to say.

I wanted to talk this over with someone. But I realized I didn't have anyone to call.

Except Philomena.

It was sort of crazy, but I didn't even know how to get in touch with her. I answered honestly.

```
GraceS_Full: I don't know what
             to say. It's really
             nice of you to give me
             the choice. Especially
             after all the awful
             things I said to you.
```

No answer for a long time.

```
JackFlash88: Yeah, it is nice of me.
             You were really nasty.
```

I cringed.

```
GraceS_Full: Sorry.

JackFlash88: So, what do you think?
             Does The Daily Dose go
             on Saturday night, or
             no?
```

I couldn't answer.

```
GraceS_Full: Can I think about it
             and tell you tomorrow?

JackFlash88: Sorry. If I'm going to
             get another band, I've
             got to call someone
             tonight. They'll need a
             few days' notice.
             Besides, what's to
             think about? You seemed
             pretty sure of your
             feelings the other day.
```

Well, I wasn't so sure anymore.

Why did I have to be the one to decide all this? This was too important for me to screw up. I suddenly felt like a little kid, desperately wanting someone to give me the right answer.

Of course I thought of Matt, of running into his room and asking his advice. I could usually find him there this time of night, sitting on his bed, strumming a guitar.

Sometimes he'd tease me by singing out the advice in some silly Elvis voice.

Matt, what should I do? I don't know what to tell him.

Then, out of the silence in my head, I knew what I had to do. The only choice.

GraceS_Full: You have to play Matt's music. That would have meant everything to him.

JackFlash88: Good answer.

I needed to say something more.

GraceS_Full: I know you were his best friend. I know Matt loved you. I'm sorry for being so screwed up. For the way I took it out on you.

He didn't answer and I thought he'd gotten up or gone off-line.

```
JackFlash88: We've all been in a
             really bad place. Let's
             just forget it, okay?
```

After all the awful things I'd said to him, he was forgiving me.

Jackson Turner was a pretty amazing guy. No wonder he and Matt had been best friends.

Maybe sometime down the road he'd be my friend, too.

My mother was nearly twenty minutes late picking me up at the library, but when she finally got there, I didn't mention it. Even though I was fuming after standing out in the cold, watching for her car.

What was the point of getting into it? I knew she'd been at church, setting up for the bandfest, which was only two days away. She hadn't asked me to help and of course I hadn't offered. We seemed to have an unspoken agreement to totally ignore it. Like ignoring an elephant lounging across the sofa in the living room.

"How did the tutoring go?"

"It was fine. Very enlightening." Okay, I was crabby.

I clipped my seat belt and my mother steered the car out into the traffic again. "I still have a ton of math homework to finish. A ton of everything, actually."

"We'll be home in five minutes. I just have to stop at the supermarket."

I groaned out loud. I couldn't help it.

My mother glanced at me. "I just need a few things for dinner. If you're in such a rush, you can take half the list and meet me at the checkout."

I felt another groan coming on but stifled it. As we walked into the market, she tore the list in two and handed me my half. "Here you go. Meet me at the express line. Bet I beat you."

"Mom, give me a break." I grabbed a basket and headed to the dairy section.

I scooped up a carton of eggs and a container of milk, then cruised down the cereal aisle. I grabbed a box of Toastie-Os from a high shelf, tossed it into the cart, and shoved off.

Rounding the corner, I found myself in a supermarket cart gridlock. The redheaded woman who faced me looked annoyed at first, then smiled in a surprised greeting. "Grace! How are you? How's your family?"

I smiled weakly. It was Sara's mother. "Oh . . . hi, Mrs. Kramer. How are you?"

My stammering words stopped short as Sara swung around the corner and walked up to us. She carried a large can of black bean soup. A special brand from the international foods aisle. I knew she loved the stuff and even ate it after school sometimes as a snack. You had to say one thing for Sara, she is definitely original.

We stared at each other but didn't say anything. I

watched as her blue eyes narrowed and glazed over. She turned to her mother. “Here’s the soup.”

Her mother looked puzzled. “Just put it in the basket, Sara.”

“Well . . . nice to see you, Mrs. Kramer. I’ll tell my mom you said hello.” I sounded like a squeaky mouse, but forced another smile. Then I backed up my cart, trying to steer around them.

Mrs. Kramer smiled briefly but didn’t answer. She looked at Sara. “Aren’t you going to talk to Grace?” I heard her ask in a hushed voice. “What’s going on?”

Sara shook her head, her curls flying in all directions. “Nothing . . . just . . . skip it, okay, Mom?” she whispered back.

I spotted an opening and pushed my cart past them, my eyes straight ahead.

But at the last minute, I couldn’t help glancing over at Sara. Our eyes met for a second. Instead of the cold, glassy stare I’d found there for weeks, I saw something different. She looked hurt . . . and confused. As if *she* didn’t understand why we weren’t friends anymore, so how could she explain it to her mother?

I stared straight ahead again and kept pushing. I’d thought I was past this, but a fresh pain cut right through me. I missed my friends. I was sorry for the way I’d treated them.

Philomena had told me to apologize. But I couldn’t do that. Not now. Not in the middle of the cereal aisle.

I rolled my cart over to the express checkout line and waited for my mother. She came toward me from the produce section and pulled up behind me in line.

"See, I told you we'd get done faster this way. That probably took less than five minutes."

I nodded. "Let's just get out of here already. I want to go home."

We managed to check out and pay for the groceries without seeing the Kramers again, but I kept thinking about Sara all night. I thought about Rebecca and Andy, too. But there didn't seem to be any way to reconnect with them now. No matter what Philomena had told me.

"What will you do tonight, all by yourself?"

"I'll be fine. I have a video, and my friend Philomena might come over."

"That girl with the long dark hair? She's sweet. I like her." My mother gave me an approving nod as she took a bite of her hamburger.

My parents were both eating quickly. They had to get to church early and organize everything before the bandfest started. My father had insisted all week that he'd stay home with me, but finally I'd persuaded him to go.

I knew it was important for him to be there when Matt was honored by our church, and I knew my mother wanted him to be there with her, too. It was my own choice to opt out of this event. I wasn't sure I could handle it, and I didn't want to ruin it for them.

Philomena offered to come by and hang out. I hadn't asked her, but of course she'd read my mind on that one loud and clear. I really didn't feel like being alone.

When it was time for my parents to leave, I walked them to the door.

"We won't be home late." My mother shrugged on a light jacket and draped a silk scarf around her neck. She gave me a long look that silently asked, *Are you sure you won't come?*

Then she kissed me quickly on the cheek and followed my dad out to the car.

The house felt empty and too quiet once they were gone.

I wrapped up the leftovers and stuck them in the fridge. Then I wandered from room to room, waiting for Philomena. I clicked on the TV and surfed the channels for a while, but nothing held my interest.

Finally I walked upstairs. I headed toward my room and stopped. Who was I kidding? That wasn't the room that was pulling at me like a magnet. Slowly I turned, walked to the other end of the hall, and opened the door to Matt's room. I walked in and switched on the low light by his bed. Then I sat on the edge of his mattress and looked around.

His room was starting to feel like a museum exhibit, and I wondered how long it would stay like this. Someday, I knew my parents would be ready to clean it out, to give away what they could to charity and store the rest of Matt's things in boxes someplace.

Yet I could feel something. His energy? Philomena's words had stuck in my head. I felt close to him here, that was for sure.

I wandered over to the electric guitars that stood on stands near his desk and picked up the red Fender, his favorite. It was heavy, but I hefted it up and pulled the thick, padded strap over my shoulder. A white plastic pick was stuck in the strings on top, and I pulled it out.

I swiped the pick over the strings, making a soft strumming sound.

Sound was energy, right? I'd read that somewhere. The tunes Matt had composed had come out of his head and his heart and still held his energy. His imprint—like a fingerprint, maybe.

Even if I didn't believe in God anymore, *that* was something I could believe in.

When I looked up, Philomena was standing in the doorway.

"How did you get in?" I was sure I'd locked the door after my parents went out.

"Through the front door. How else would I have done it?" She stood with her jacket still on, her car keys in her hand. There were so many questions I wanted to ask her, but they would have to wait for another time.

Seeing Philomena there and holding Matt's guitar in

my hands gave me a rush of strength I hadn't experienced in a long time. It was enough to make me feel like I could do this.

"So, ready to go?" She smiled at me, a knowing gleam in her dark eyes.

I took one more strum on the guitar, ending with a flourish.

"Yes. I am," I answered, surprising myself.

We didn't talk much on the way over. My stomach jumped with nerves while Philomena seemed, as usual, unnaturally calm.

Even on Christmas Eve I'd never seen so many cars at the church. They filled the parking lot and lined the street for blocks. As unlikely as it seemed, Philomena found a parking spot right in front. I wasn't all that surprised.

We paid at the door and eased our way into the crowd. The building was packed. Everywhere I looked, I saw familiar faces: members of our church, neighbors, friends of our family, friends of my mother's from work, and lots of people my father knew in town or through his business. I even saw teachers and so many kids I knew, it could have been a school dance.

The back of the Fellowship Hall had been set up with a big stage. A long banner across the back curtain read: MATTHEW D. STANLEY MEMORIAL CONCERT.

I stared up at it, a catch in my throat.

The group onstage was slamming away at their guitars, the lead singer shouting into the microphone as they finished up a tune. It wasn't Matt's band, just the warm-up act. We hadn't missed too much.

"I can't believe this place. I've never seen it so full." I had to lean close to Philomena so she could hear me.

"Everybody loved Matt. Everyone wants to honor his memory."

I nodded, unable to answer her. I'd been so wrong to say I wouldn't come here. So stubborn and selfish. I was glad I'd changed my mind—or Matt had changed it for me.

I turned to Philomena again. "Thanks for bringing me here."

"No thanks necessary." She squeezed my arm and smiled.

I wanted to find my parents, but it was impossible to see farther than two feet ahead. I edged my way up toward the stage, hoping to spot them.

The song ended, and the audience clapped and cheered as the band took some bows. Then I saw the members of Matt's band walk out onstage. They adjusted their instruments and equipment, then took their positions, looking very serious.

Jackson came out last. He slipped his guitar strap over his shoulder and leaned toward the microphone.

He looked extremely cool, wearing a shiny black suit jacket over a white T-shirt and torn-up jeans. His hair was spiked up in front, but just the right amount.

"We are The Daily Dose, and we're glad to be here tonight. We want to thank everyone who put this event together."

The audience burst into applause, cheering and screaming so loudly I could hardly hear him.

"All the songs we're about to play were written by Matt Stanley. We wouldn't be here if it wasn't for Matt. He started this band to give the world some good music, and he made us work hard to play it right."

Jackson's words sounded thick and choked, and he bowed his head a second, struggling to finish what he had to say. Then he looked out somewhere high above the audience.

"We miss you, Matt. We love you, man."

The band hit the opening notes of their first song, "Down to the Wire." Tears that I'd been holding back filled my eyes. The band blurred, but the music filled my head.

I closed my eyes and gave myself over to the sound. Before I could stop myself, I heard the words in my head. *Thank you for this. Thanks . . . God.*

I opened my eyes and looked for Philomena. But she wasn't standing next to me anymore. She was gone.

The Daily Dose played for more than an hour: fast songs, slow songs, funny songs, wise ones, too. I'd never realized how many great tunes Matt had created. It was sad to think there would be no more, but he'd managed to achieve a lot in his short time.

The place went wild. Maybe in the back of my mind I'd expected this event to be somber and bleak, like a funeral service with electric guitars.

But it was just the opposite, a raucous celebration of Matt's life, his music, the love he gave so freely to everyone who knew him. His short, sweet life. I felt his spirit fill the place, just blowing the roof off.

After the band played their last encore and took their final bows, Pastor James came onstage.

He spoke about the homeless shelter the church was setting up, how it would help so many people, even save lives in the coldest part of winter, and give so much back to the community.

"It seemed only fitting to us that a project like this should be dedicated to the memory of a young man we all loved so much. His talent and beautiful spirit live on here tonight, touching our hearts and souls, as he touched everyone who knew him.

"I'm going to call his family up here to join me, and I hope you will welcome them."

Pastor James walked to the edge of the stage, gesturing into the crowd below. I stood on tiptoe and could see just the back of my parents' heads and people nearby them persuading them to go up onstage.

I knew my mother especially hated attention. But she deserved applause tonight. She deserved so much more than that.

They were finally onstage standing next to our pastor,

when somebody shouted out, "Grace . . . Grace Stanley is here, too! Back there!"

A few people pointed to me, and all heads turned. My parents looked shocked, especially my father. I thought he might faint and do an unintentional body crash into the audience.

A girl's voice whispered close to my ear. "Go ahead, Grace. You should be up there, too."

I turned, thinking I'd see Philomena. But it was Rebecca! Andy and Sara stood right behind her. They were all watching me, but with warmth in their eyes.

"Do you want me to go with you?" Rebecca asked.

"Would you?"

Rebecca took hold of my arm, and The Wall started working her way through the crowd. Andy and Sara followed closely behind.

We reached the stage. I turned to the three of them. "Thanks . . . See you guys later?"

"We'll look for you," Rebecca promised. "Now get up there."

I still had plenty of explaining and apologizing to do. But I had a feeling this time they would listen.

I walked across the stage to my parents, and my dad put his arm around my shoulders and pulled me close. He was laughing and crying at the same time and so was I.

"And now I wish to honor someone who has given so much of herself, working hard to make tonight's event and our new shelter a reality: Brenda Stanley."

Pastor James turned to my mother, and she bowed her head modestly.

The crowd burst into applause, and even the pastor's calming hand motions could hardly stop the clapping several moments later.

Then a girl from the youth group ran out from backstage carrying two huge bouquets. She handed one bunch to my mother—and one to me.

I stood speechless, staring down at the velvety red flowers, one more beautiful than the next, each so perfectly formed. All I could think about was what Philomena had told me about miracles, how they unfold like roses.

There they were, right in my arms.

Roses.

Something had happened to me tonight. A miracle, or as close to one as I'd ever come. I felt connected again—to my family, to my friends . . . to Matt.

Even to God.

I scanned the crowd, looking for Philomena. Where had she gone? Had she left already?

No, there she was. My eyes rested on her familiar face, her shining dark eyes and warm smile.

The smile that said so plainly, *You screw up sometimes, Grace. But I love you anyway.*

It was hard to get up for church the next morning, but we all managed. I was the surprise factor. When I came down dressed and ready, my parents both looked amazed but didn't dare say anything.

After the service we went into the Fellowship Hall to help the youth group with the last of the cleanup. Then I was going into town to meet up with Rebecca, Andy, and Sara for coffee. We had some catching up to do.

The cleanup didn't take very long, many hands making light work and all of that.

I was carrying some folding chairs back into the sanctuary, stumbling a bit since I'd taken too many at once.

Someone tapped my shoulder. "Here, let me help you with those."

Before I could answer, Philomena had taken half the load and was carrying the chairs toward the choir room. Though I'd never told her that's where they had to go.

"Thanks. Is this part of your job description, too?"

"It's very open-ended." She rested the chairs against the wall and brushed off her hands.

I put my chairs onto the pile, and we walked back into the sanctuary together.

The sanctuary was silent and dim, amber- and rose-colored shafts of light filtering through the stained-glass window behind the altar. Even though we spoke quietly, our voices echoed in the empty space.

"I want to show you something." I sat down and pulled my sketchbook out of my purse. I flipped it open to the drawing I'd made of her. It was finally finished.

I'd been so wired after the concert, I hadn't been able to sleep. I'd picked up my sketchbook, and it fell open to Philomena's portrait. I began drawing, filling in the missing parts of the sketch with a piece of charcoal. Drawing felt the way it used to before Matt's death: fluid and smooth, one line flowing into the next, as if at every moment the charcoal knew exactly where it was supposed to be. As if I were drawing it in a dream.

When I woke up in the morning and found the book open on the floor by my bed, I barely remembered working on it. But there it was, Philomena's image captured perfectly—more than just the girl people saw wandering around the halls at school. I'd somehow captured something inside of her, that strange, warm light that seemed to shine from her eyes and her heart.

Philomena sat beside me and looked at the drawing. "Wow . . . that's wonderful." She looked so pleased. "Nobody has ever drawn my portrait before."

"Would you like to keep it?" I asked.

It was the first real drawing I'd completed in months. One of the best I'd ever done. But I was happy to give it to her. It seemed like such a small gift. She'd already given me so much.

"Are you sure?"

I nodded. "Absolutely. It's sort of a gift. For helping me. Thank you."

She smiled again. "You're welcome, but we're not done yet. We work well together, Grace. This is just the beginning. I'm going to keep helping . . . if you'll let me."

I slowly pulled the page out, careful not to tear the edges. "So, tell me something. Who are you? Really." I held out the sketch and she took it. "Are you an angel or something?"

She tilted her head to one side. "Something like that."

"No, really," I pressed. "What are you? An angel? A saint?"

The corners of her mouth turned up. "Well, I don't have wings, or a halo, or beams of light coming out of my head, but—"

"You're serious. You're actually from somewhere . . . else?"

She nodded. "The title isn't important. I've been sent here to help you," Philomena said, her voice light and easy.

I felt wobbly all over. The roses were real. I had no doubt that miracles existed. But to believe what she was telling me . . .

"Why me?"

"Why not you?"

We were going back into one of our circular conversations, but that no longer seemed so strange. It was actually beginning to make some kind of sense.

"Do you believe me?" she asked.

It was so quiet in the sanctuary that I thought I could hear my own heart beat.

I nodded slowly. "Yes. Yes, I do."

She smiled at me and touched my hand. A strange warmth flowed through my veins.

For the first time in months—maybe for the first time in my life—I was filled with peace. And stillness.

I felt love, in me and outside me. I knew Philomena loved me and that God loved me, too. I remembered what Philomena had said about Matt's being near, and even though I couldn't see him, I *felt* him. It was as if I would see him if I turned my head quickly enough.

But I didn't turn my head. I sat looking at the altar and the high, arching beams—content to know we would always be connected, Matt and me.

I felt connected . . . to everything.

Finally I turned and looked at Philomena. I was almost afraid to ask, but I had to. "How are you going to keep helping me? I mean, things aren't going to get worse again before they get better, are they?"

She smiled, nearly laughing at me. "Don't worry. You'll see."

"I'll see what?" I asked skeptically.

"You have a gift. You're going to help me reach out to others. Change their lives for the better."

"You mean with the shelter, here at church?"

"Oh, sure. But I mean more than that, too."

I shook my head. "I'm so screwy lately, I can't get out of my own way. How am I going to help anybody else?"

"Things take time to unfold, remember?" Then she just smiled, that slow, peaceful smile of hers.

I knew better by now than to argue with Philomena. She always had the last word.

Even when she wasn't saying a thing.